PHILIP ALLAN

LITERATURE GUIDE

FOR A-LEVEL

THE WINTER'S TALE
WILLIAM SHAKESPEARE

Pete Bunten and Peter Malin

Series editor: Nicola Onyett

PHILIP ALLAN
UPDATES

Philip Allan Updates, an imprint of Hodder Education, an Hachette UK company, Market Place, Deddington, Oxfordshire OX15 0SE

Orders

Bookpoint Ltd, 130 Milton Park, Abingdon, Oxfordshire OX14 4SB
tel: 01235 827827
fax: 01235 400401
e-mail: education@bookpoint.co.uk
Lines are open 9.00 a.m.–5.00 p.m., Monday to Saturday, with a 24-hour message answering service. You can also order through the Philip Allan Updates website: www.philipallan.co.uk

© Pete Bunten and Peter Malin

ISBN 978-1-4441-1792-9

First printed 2010

Impression number 5 4 3 2 1

Year 2014 2013 2012 2011 2010

Printed in Spain

Hachette UK's policy is to use papers that are natural, renewable and recyclable products and made from wood grown in sustainable forests. The logging and manufacturing processes are expected to conform to the environmental regulations of the country of origin.

Cover photo © Olly/Fotolia

Contents

Using this guide

Why read this guide?

The purposes of this A-level Literature Guide are to enable you to organise your thoughts and responses to the text, deepen your understanding of key features and aspects and help you to address the particular requirements of examination questions and coursework tasks in order to obtain the best possible grade. It will also prove useful to those of you writing a coursework piece on the text as it provides a number of summaries, lists, analyses and references to help with the content and construction of the assignment.

Note that teachers and examiners are seeking above all else evidence of an *informed personal response to the text*. A guide such as this can help you to understand the text, form your own opinions, and suggest areas to think about, but it cannot replace your own ideas and responses as an informed and autonomous reader.

Line references in the guide refer to the Cambridge School Shakespeare edition of *The Winter's Tale*, edited by Sheila Innes and Elizabeth Huddlestone (Cambridge University Press, 1999). If you are using another edition, the references should be easy enough to find, although there will inevitably be a few lines' difference in scenes containing prose. References to other plays by Shakespeare are to the Oxford *Complete Works*, compact edition, edited by Stanley Wells and Gary Taylor (Clarendon Press, 1988). In referring to modern performances of the play, the initials 'RSC' stand for the Royal Shakespeare Company. Dates given refer to the year in which a particular production opened.

How to make the most of this guide

You may find it useful to read sections of this guide when you need them, rather than reading it from start to finish. For example, you may find it helpful to read the *Contexts* section before you start reading the text, or to read the *Scene summaries and commentaries* section in conjunction with the text — whether to back up your first reading of it at school or college or to help you revise. The sections relating to the Assessment Objectives will be especially useful in the weeks leading up to the exam.

Key elements

Look at the **Context** boxes to find interesting facts that are relevant to the text.

Be exam-ready

Broaden your thinking about the text by answering the questions in the **Pause for Thought** boxes. These help you to consider your own opinions in order to develop your skills of criticism and analysis.

Pause for **Thought**

Build critical skills

Taking it Further boxes suggest poems, films, etc. that provide further background or illuminating parallels to the text.

Taking it **Further**

Where to find out more

Use the **Task** boxes to develop your understanding of the text and test your knowledge of it. Answers for some of the tasks are given online, and do not forget to look online for further self-tests on the text.

Task

Test yourself

A cross-reference to a **Top ten quotation** (see pages 88–91 of this guide), where each quotation is accompanied by a commentary that shows why it is important.

❮ Top ten **quotation**

Know your text

Don't forget to go online: **www.philipallan.co.uk/literatureguidesonline** where you can find additional exam responses, a glossary of literary terms, interactive questions, podcasts and much more.

Synopsis

Polixenes, the king of Bohemia, has for nine months been the guest of his life-long friend, Leontes, the king of Sicilia. Leontes attempts to persuade his friend to extend his stay, but it is only when Hermione, the queen, adds her voice that Polixenes agrees to remain. At this point Leontes is seized by a sudden and uncontrollable frenzy of jealousy. He convinces himself not only that Polixenes and Hermione are lovers but also that his heavily pregnant wife is carrying Polixenes' child. Leontes refuses to listen to the advice of his principal adviser, the Lord Camillo, and in a fury commands Camillo to poison Polixenes.

Camillo cannot bring himself to commit such an act, however, and fearful for his own and Polixenes' safety, arranges their escape from Sicilia. Leontes takes their flight as confirmation of his suspicions and sends Hermione to prison where she gives birth to a daughter. Paulina, a lady of the court, brings the child from the prison to the king, hoping to convince him that the queen is innocent and that he is the true father of the child. Leontes disowns the child and orders Paulina's husband, Antigonus, to take the baby to some wild and deserted place and leave it there to fate and the elements.

Hermione is then brought to trial. The king has sent servants to Delphos, to consult Apollo's oracle, in order to obtain what Leontes believes will be the final proof of Hermione's guilt. At her trial Hermione defends herself courageously and places her trust in the word of the oracle. The oracle proclaims that she is innocent, the king has acted tyrannously, and he will live without an heir until what has been lost is found. Leontes furiously denounces the oracle and immediately news is brought of his son's sudden death. The queen faints and is carried away. Leontes is consumed by grief and remorse, but Paulina returns to the court to announce that Hermione has died. The grief-stricken king vows to spend the rest of his life in repentance and mourning.

Meanwhile Antigonus has travelled by boat to Bohemia where he has been told in a dream to abandon the child. He and his crew suffer dreadful deaths, but the baby girl, now named Perdita, survives and is found by a local Shepherd and his son.

Sixteen years pass and we meet Perdita again, now the adopted daughter of the Shepherd and about to act as hostess at a sheep-shearing feast. She has met and fallen in love with Florizel, the son of the Bohemian king, Polixenes. He has kept his love affair secret from his father but

Polixenes and Camillo arrive at the feast and the king angrily forbids their planned marriage. Camillo, however, longs to see Sicilia again, and he organises the young couple's escape by sea, partially aided by the rogue and pedlar, Autolycus.

The Shepherd and his son have been prevented from telling Polixenes the truth about Perdita's origins, and they and the king follow in pursuit to Sicilia. The arrival of Florizel and Perdita brings joy to the Sicilian court and to Leontes, still locked in bitter penitence and mourning for his dead queen. Leontes agrees to speak to Polixenes on the young couple's behalf, and, on the arrival of the Bohemian party, a general reconciliation takes place. Paulina then takes the company to her house to view a remarkable statue of Hermione. Awe-struck, they see the statue apparently come to life. It is revealed that Hermione hid herself away in the hope that the words of the oracle would come true. Now that Perdita has been found, she can live again. The play ends in general celebration and the promise of more than one marriage.

Scene summaries and commentaries

As with all parts of this guide, you should use this section critically. It is not a substitute for your own close reading of the text: there are other angles and interpretations which are not considered here. Question everything you read and weigh it against your own understanding of each scene. The commentary in particular is highly selective. It cannot cover every aspect of every scene, and the focus here is usually on character, themes, language and elements of drama.

Act I scene 1

Archidamus, in conversation with Camillo, praises the hospitality the Bohemian visitors have received in the Sicilian court, and doubts if his own country could match it if a return visit were paid. They discuss the longstanding friendship of their kings, dating from childhood, and the admirable qualities of the young Sicilian prince, Mamillius, who inspires the people with a sense of wellbeing.

Commentary: **Opening scenes are crucial in imparting important background information to the audience. Shakespeare often begins, as here, with two subsidiary characters discussing the social and political situation. Archidamus remains anonymous in the dialogue and never reappears, whereas Camillo develops into a major supporting character throughout the play. Archidamus is thus a dramatic device rather than a fully developed character.**

Camillo and Archidamus converse in courtly prose. Their discourse is polite, artificial and rhetorical, full of verbal flourishes such as false modesty and hyperbole, as when Archidamus suggests that, if the Sicilians were to visit Bohemia, their hosts would have to drug them to conceal the inadequacy of their hospitality. The polite surface of their polished prose forms a striking contrast with the passionate and emotional verse that is to be released in the next scene.

As well as imparting information, Shakespeare uses the opening scene to establish some of the play's key images. In particular, the central opposition of youth and old age is explored through

the account of Leontes' and Polixenes' childhood friendship, and through the curative power of Mamillius to make 'old hearts fresh' (lines 31–32). Retrospectively, however, the discussion is invested with a sad irony in view of Mamillius's subsequent fate. There is irony, too, in Camillo's plea for 'the heavens' to 'continue' the love between Polixenes and Leontes (line 25), and Archidamus's forcefully alliterative reply that there is neither 'malice or matter' in the world to alter it (line 26).

Task 1

Explore some different ways in which this scene could be staged to assist what might seem an undramatic opening.

Leontes, Hermione and Polixenes in a production at the Old Vic Theatre in 2009

Act I scene 2

After nine months in Sicilia, Polixenes is anxious to return home, but Leontes tries to talk him into extending his visit, if only by a few days. At Leontes' request, Hermione, who is in the late stages of pregnancy, joins in his attempts at persuasion, and is soon successful. Leontes praises Hermione's powers of persuasion; however, he is overcome with jealousy, even seeking reassurance from Mamillius that he is indeed his son. Leontes sends Mamillius off to play and engages Camillo in conversation, demanding to know his thoughts on Hermione's success in getting Polixenes to stay longer. Camillo is astonished by Leontes' assertions of Hermione's infidelity and vigorously defends her, but responds equivocally to the king's demand that he poison Polixenes. He eventually promises to do it providing no action is subsequently taken against the queen. Left alone, Camillo determines to disobey the king and abandon the court; he reluctantly tells everything to Polixenes, who has returned wondering why Leontes has just pointedly ignored him. Camillo urges Polixenes to escape while he has the chance, and pledges his services to him.

Commentary: **The pace of this long scene is impressively swift, moving with gripping intensity from domestic harmony to disruption and fragmentation. The language of Leontes' jealous outbursts is passionate and violent, providing a striking contrast with both the calm, measured fluency of Polixenes and Hermione's lively and attractive wit. In Leontes' speeches, the verse rhythms are often irregular and fractured, the grammatical structures complicated and parenthetical. Even so, the beat of the iambic pentameter still powerfully underlies the verse in regular lines such as 'To mingle friendship far is mingling bloods' (line 109), often emphasised, as here, by repetition. Alliterative effects combine with assonance to create the onomatopoeic spitting and hissing of his intemperate passion: 'paddling palms and pinching fingers' (line 115); 'Inch-thick, knee-deep' (line 186); 'whose issue/Will hiss me to my grave' (lines 188–89); 'sluiced in's absence' (line 194) .**

With such an intense focus on Leontes, it is easy to overlook the other characters, stereotyping them merely as models of virtue. It is certainly important that we are in no doubt about Hermione's integrity, which is emphatically presented through the Christian terminology of 'grace'. The word itself is on her lips three times in the space of 25 lines, while both Camillo and Polixenes refer to her as 'gracious'. Yet she does not have to be presented as a paragon, and an actor can make her more human by stressing a slightly irritating quality in some of her bantering wit.

It is easy, too, to take Polixenes and Camillo at face value, when perhaps Shakespeare subtly invites us to question certain aspects of their behaviour. If, for example, Polixenes loves his young son so much, how can he justify having abandoned him, not to mention his country, for nine months? 'My affairs/Do even drag me homeward' (lines 23–24), he says, the language suggesting a reluctance to resume his responsibilities. Also, what are we to make of Camillo's and Polixenes' flight from danger at the end of the scene? Instead of confronting Leontes, or warning Hermione, they leave her to her fate.

Top ten *quotation*

*Pause for **Thought***

How convincing do you find the idea that Polixenes and Camillo do not have to be presented wholly positively?

8

This scene is dense with powerfully emotive patterns of imagery, of which the most noticeable is perhaps the idea of disease. From the 'tremor cordis' that Leontes experiences at the outbreak of his jealousy, he sees his imagined transformation into a cuckold, his brow sprouting that creature's horns, in terms of an 'infection' of his brains, and comments that thousands of husbands 'Have the disease and feel't not' (line 207). For him, the origin of the disease lies in Hermione's supposed infidelity: 'Were my wife's liver/Infected as her life, she would not live/The running of one glass' (lines 304–06).

The image of the hourglass here connects with another important strand of imagery developed in the scene through its frequent references to time, later to be given concrete embodiment in the Act IV chorus. From units of time — 'Nine changes of the wat'ry star', 'One sev'night', 'a month', 'a week', 'hours', 'minutes' — to specific moments — 'tomorrow', 'today', 'noon', midnight'; from the clocks and hourglasses that measure time, to the concept of 'perpetuity' and eternity, time's controlling power in human life is stressed.

Disease, though, remains the more noticeable idea in the scene, and when it is taken up by Camillo and Polixenes in a number of references stressing its infectious quality, its origin is firmly located in Leontes' jealous obsession. At present there is no remedy, despite Camillo's urging of Leontes to 'be cured/ Of this diseased opinion' (lines 296–97). There is, however, a potential cure, which in the first part of the play is impotent and inoperative, embodied in the power of childhood innocence. Employing the seasonal imagery which is also so important in the overall scheme of the play, Polixenes states that his young son:

> ...makes a July's day short as December,
> And with his varying childness cures in me
> Thoughts that would thick my blood.　　　　(lines 169–71)

❮ Top ten *quotation*

In response, Leontes claims that Mamillius has the same effect on him: 'So stands this squire/Officed with me' (lines 171–72); a remark that is filled with a sad and profound irony, since the child is clearly exerting no such curative power on his father's obsessive jealousy.

In subtle touches, Shakespeare anticipates his later presentation of Bohemia as essentially a pastoral economy through incidental images in the speech of Polixenes, from his reference to 'the

Context

The reflections on childhood and maturity are often seen in terms of innocence and experience. Growing into adulthood is defined by Polixenes as an increasing awareness of sin, and his discussion with Hermione between lines 67 and 86 is crammed with suggestions of evil and temptation, sin and guilt, referring explicitly to the biblical doctrine of original sin. These Christian references have led some commentators to interpret the whole play in the light of Christian theology.

Pause for **Thought**

The speed and suddenness with which Leontes' jealousy takes hold have aroused centuries of critical debate. An actor needs to decide whether Leontes is already jealous before Act I scene 2 begins, or whether his suspicions descend on him as the action unfolds. (NB: the argument that this latter view is psychologically unconvincing should acknowledge that characters in plays need not behave as people do in real life.) What is your reading of this aspect of the scene?

shepherd's note' in his opening speech to his comparison of Leontes and himself as children to 'twinned lambs'. In more ominous hints of later developments, Shakespeare two or three times uses images of imprisonment, anticipating Hermione's imminent incarceration.

This is a rich and complex scene, overlaying its dramatic events with webs and patterns of suggestive imagery, only a few examples of which have been dealt with in this commentary.

Act II scene 1

Unaware of imminent disaster, Hermione and her ladies are entertained by Mamillius's childish prattle. Leontes receives news of Camillo's and Polixenes' flight, which he interprets as confirmation of his suspicions. He removes Mamillius from Hermione and accuses her publicly of adultery with Polixenes, who he claims is the father of her unborn child. She denies it, refutes his accusations with dignity and submits herself both to his commands and to the operation of heavenly providence. She and her ladies are escorted to prison, while Antigonus and other lords are left to plead on her behalf and forcefully defend her innocence. To placate them, Leontes says he has already sent Cleomenes and Dion to seek confirmation of Hermione's guilt from the oracle of Apollo at Delphos.

Commentary: **This is a shocking scene, which derives its power largely from Leontes' violent disruption of domestic harmony and his public shaming of his wife. It carries a similar dramatic impact to Othello's equally public humiliation of Desdemona, and removes all trace of sympathy from the king. Yet there is also an almost comic lack of authority in Leontes' failure to stifle his lords' criticisms of his actions, and Antigonus's forthrightness is the play's first real corrective to the king's increasingly deranged fantasies. Antigonus's promise to 'geld' his daughters if Hermione is 'honour-flawed' is not so much a horrifying demonstration of patriarchal power as a comic hyperbole that confirms his faith in the queen. Antigonus's concluding lines set the seal on Leontes' potential as comic fool, and point to an outcome which, ironically, he does not survive to witness.**

In the opening section of the scene, Shakespeare deftly sketches in the secure and loving relationships centred on Hermione and Mamillius. Her pregnancy is discussed by the ladies in warmly colloquial phrases: 'The queen your mother rounds apace' (line

16); 'She is spread of late/Into a goodly bulk' (lines 19–20). Mamillius himself is a typical Shakespearean child character, and to modern tastes he can appear irritatingly spoilt and knowing, like the doomed youngsters in other plays such as *Richard III* and *Macbeth*. His abortive story-telling, however, marks a key point in the play, invoking its title explicitly in his introductory comment, 'A sad tale's best for winter' (line 25). 'Tale' suggests something fanciful, to be taken with a pinch of salt, yet to see the whole play in this light is to diminish its essential seriousness. The 'sprites and goblins' of the tale are perhaps suggestive of the demons of jealousy that torment his father, whom one might identify as the man who 'dwelt by a churchyard', in the sense that he is to spend 16 years of his life visiting the chapel where lie the bodies of Mamillius himself and, as he thinks, Hermione.

Visually, this touching domestic scene continues to one side of the stage, enhancing the ominous dramatic power of Leontes' conversation with the lords on the other side, before the warm bond between mother and child is disrupted by his violent incursion. Compared with Hermione's quiet and measured dignity, Leontes' explosive language, with its alliteration and other repetitive sound effects, suggests a mind both tortured and unbalanced. Its impact, however, is weak, not authoritative, as he perhaps realises in adopting a more controlled, if self-righteous, tone in explaining that he has already sought confirmation of Hermione's guilt from Apollo's oracle since, as he says with unconscious comic irony, 'in an act of this importance 'twere/ Most piteous to be wild' (lines 181–82). By the end of the scene, a number of dramatic expectations have been set up, including the tension of Hermione's imprisonment when she is so near to childbirth and the outcome of the mission to Delphos.

Task 2

Some significant dramatic contrasts in this scene have been indicated above. Find examples of others that you consider important.

Act II scene 2

Prevented from speaking to the imprisoned queen in person, Paulina is allowed access to her lady, Emilia, who tells her that Hermione has given birth to a daughter. They agree that Paulina will take the child to the king in the hope that it will have a positive influence on him. The gaoler is at first reluctant to release the child, but Paulina persuades him that he has no legal reason to detain it, and promises to protect him from any repercussions.

Context

Shakespeare lived in a patriarchal society, and the women's roles in his plays were taken by boys. So his treatment of the female characters in the play is interesting, and he seems to use them both to exploit and challenge traditional female stereotypes. In the previous scene, for example, Hermione drew attention to the stereotype of the emotional woman by the very act of denying its validity in herself: 'I am not prone to weeping, as our sex/Commonly are' (II.1.108–09).

Commentary: **Paulina is a striking new character: assertive, forthright, determined, resourceful and fiercely loyal to Hermione.**

Paulina seems to present herself as the stereotype of the scold, declaring that the king 'must be told' and that 'The office/ Becomes a woman best' (lines 31–32). Her two references to her tongue confirm the convention of the nagging, shrewish woman: 'If I prove honey-mouthed, let my tongue blister' (line 33), and 'I'll use that tongue I have' (line 52). Ironically, though, she also acknowledges that the image of the child itself may prove more effective, since 'The silence often of pure innocence/Persuades when speaking fails' (lines 41–42).

Shakespeare invariably takes considerable care in creating smaller roles, and there are two typical examples in this scene. Like Paulina, Emilia is loyal and protective towards the queen, and her verse is measured and dignified. There is almost a sense of a supportive sisterhood at work on Hermione's behalf, and Shakespeare imbues Emilia's language with the imagery of virtue, both homely, in terms such as 'goodly' and 'lusty'; and more abstract, in words like 'worthy', 'honour', 'goodness', 'noble' and 'blest'. There is irony in her optimism, though, which perhaps we notice even if we do not know the outcome, when Emilia tells Paulina, 'your free undertaking cannot miss/A thriving issue' (lines 44–45). Such confidence proves to be misplaced, at least in the short term.

The gaoler, too, is deftly characterised, as a man whose moral scruples are in conflict with his job, first in admitting Paulina to the queen, which he avoids by letting her speak with Emilia, and then in allowing the baby to be taken away. He covers his back by insisting on remaining present during the women's conversation, but ultimately gives in to Paulina's 'honour' — a word spoken five times in this short scene.

Act II scene 3

Racked by sleeplessness, Leontes reflects on Mamillius's sudden illness, which he blames on Hermione's shameful behaviour. Paulina, with the baby, forces her way into the chamber despite the protestations of the lords. Ignoring Leontes' commands to have her ejected, she presents the baby to him, berates him for his treatment of Hermione, refutes his protestations that he is not the child's father by drawing attention to its likeness to him, and departs, leaving the baby princess behind. Blaming Antigonus for his wife's behaviour, Leontes instructs him to see the child burned to death. Responding to the lords' pleas for mercy, however, he orders Antigonus to take the baby to some foreign shore and there abandon it. Reluctantly, and with compassion, Antigonus leaves with the child as a servant arrives with news that Cleomenes and Dion have returned from the oracle at Delphos. Leontes orders Hermione's trial to be arranged, though to him the outcome is a foregone conclusion.

Commentary: **This powerful scene, centring on the confrontation between Leontes and Paulina, with the baby as its visual focus, is both serious and comic in its impact. Leontes' sleeplessness is viewed as a symptom of the disease caused by his intemperate jealousy which affects him and his son. Paulina claims to offer him a cure as his 'physician'.**

Leontes' treatment of Paulina in this scene continually plays on a set of contemporary misogynist stereotypes of women who step outside their subservient position in society. As Antigonus's wife, Paulina should bow to his control, so her independent behaviour gives Leontes ample opportunity for a series of sarcastic jibes at the old lord's expense: 'Canst not rule her?' (line 46) he demands, accusing him of being 'woman-tired', or hen-pecked. Antigonus, though, is quite happy to accept the reversed gender roles in his marriage, commenting ruefully, 'When she will take the rein, I let her run' (line 51). Much of the scene's deflationary humour comes from this relationship, and when Leontes suggests that Antigonus is 'worthy to be hanged' for his failure to keep his wife quiet, his comic response, 'Hang all the husbands/That cannot do that feat, you'll leave yourself/Hardly one subject' (lines 109–11) reveals a wry awareness of life.

It is Leontes who consigns Paulina to the stereotype of the scold, through a series of insulting phrases: 'a mankind witch', 'a most intelligencing bawd'. The scene however, challenges these anti-feminist stereotypes since it is Paulina who is clearly in the right. Furthermore, in appealing again to 'good goddess Nature', Paulina aligns herself with those positive forces which are promoted later in the play, as opposed to the unnaturalness of the witch or the masculine woman that Leontes would have her be.

It is, rather, Leontes who is behaving unnaturally, something that is revealed through the language he uses to refer to the child. While Paulina and the lords refer to the baby in

compassionate terms as 'daughter', 'princess', 'babe', 'poor babe' or 'the innocent', Leontes repeatedly uses demeaning terms such as 'bastard', 'brat' or 'issue', consistently employing the pronoun 'it' to dehumanise the child he refuses to acknowledge as his.

Paulina demonstrates a range of qualities during the scene, including outspoken resistance to Leontes' threats to have her 'burnt', when she asserts that 'It is an heretic that makes the fire,/Not she which burns in't' (lines 114–15), and physical courage in the face of the men's weak attempts to remove her forcibly — 'I pray you do not push me' (line 124); 'What needs these hands?' (line 126). It is thus easy to overlook her grave error of judgement, perhaps even her moral culpability, in leaving the baby to Leontes' mercy.

Pause for **Thought** ❙❙

How convincing do you find the idea that Leontes often seems as much a comic as a tragic figure in the first two acts?

Act III scene 1

Having returned from Delphos, Cleomenes and Dion reflect on their experiences there, and hope that the oracle will prove advantageous to Hermione.

Commentary: **Unnecessary to the structure of both narrative and plot, this scene is nonetheless crucial in our response to the play, offering, as it does, a breath of linguistic fresh air. The Sicilian court has become so claustrophobic, so bound up with images of disease and imprisonment, that it is a relief to sense that there is a world elsewhere, imbued with a sense of transcendent moral virtue and a power other than that of Leontes' obsessive tyranny. It needs little more than a listing of some of the scene's key adjectives — 'delicate', 'sweet', 'fertile', 'celestial', 'ceremonious', 'solemn', 'unearthly', 'rare', 'pleasant', 'fresh' and 'gracious' — to demonstrate the effect Shakespeare wants it to create.**

Pause for **Thought** ❙❙

What would be lost from the play if this scene were omitted in performance?

Act III scene 2

At her trial, Hermione offers a dignified and eloquent self-defence. The oracle is opened and read: it declares Hermione innocent and condemns Leontes to live without an heir unless the lost child is found. As the king denounces the oracle, a servant enters to announce the death of Mamillius, at which the queen faints and is escorted out. Leontes is overcome with repentance, but Paulina returns to report that Hermione has also died. Leontes accepts Paulina's rebukes, asks to be shown the bodies of his queen and son, and promises daily penance at their tomb.

Commentary: **This scene offers a fast-moving sequence of dramatic events and unexpected reverses of fortune. Shakespeare now excludes all traces of comedy, so that the overall impact is tragic and moving. Indeed, the scene could well mark the conclusion of a short tragedy, were it not for the 'if' in the oracle's verdict that suggests further potential developments.**

As he opens the trial, Leontes seems calm and controlled, and his language is formal and restrained. Revealingly, he uses the royal plural in his opening speech, to distance himself from personal responsibility and involvement, and appeals for respect by talking of his love for Hermione, his 'great grief' at the necessity of a trial, and his even-handed determination to pursue 'justice', whether represented by his wife's 'guilt or...purgation'. It is not long before his veneer of reason and restraint breaks down, however, and by his speech at line 80 he has reverted to abuse, returning to the intemperate accusations of his jealous rage and referring to the baby once more as 'bastard' and 'brat'. When he now talks of justice, it is clear that the word, for him, represents only the proof of Hermione's guilt: 'so thou/Shalt feel our justice, in whose easiest passage/Look for no less than death' (lines 87–89). Justice, however, is impartial, and the oracle declares Hermione, Polixenes and Camillo to be innocent. The concept is complicated, though, by the fact that Leontes' punishment is marked by the entirely unjust deaths visited upon his son and, as it appears, his wife. Unjust actions such as his, Shakespeare seems to be suggesting, have repercussions on the guilty and the innocent alike.

During her trial, Hermione is an impressive figure on stage, whether she is made to appear upright and queenly or, ravaged by her imprisonment, weak and hardly able to stand. It is the eloquence of her language that invests her with nobility and dignity. Unlike Leontes, she does not take refuge in the royal plural, but centres her argument on the singular personal pronoun and its variants — 'I', 'me', 'my', 'mine' — since it is her own 'integrity' that is under attack. She confines herself largely to the statement of known facts: her previously acknowledged virtue, her present unhappiness and the shame of her public trial. She adds to this, however, a faith in 'powers divine', a courageous attack on 'tyranny', an assertion that she prizes her honour above her life and a simple denial of any dishonourable behaviour. With bitter resignation she sums up, 'Tell me what

*Pause for **Thought***

It has been argued by Susan Powell that *The Winter's Tale* cannot ultimately be seen as a tragedy because of its emphasis on healing and renewal. What do you think of this view?

*Pause for **Thought***

In David Farr's 2009 RSC production, Hermione appeared at her trial in what the critic Michael Billington described as 'blood-streaked post-natal robes'. Discuss the impact you think this image would have created.

blessings I have here alive/That I should fear to die' (lines 105–06).

The turning point of the scene comes with the reading of the oracle, Leontes' denunciation of it, the immediate announcement of Mamillius's death, the king's sudden repentance, and the removal of the swooning Hermione. All of this happens within 25 lines of spoken text, and shows Shakespeare to be fully in control of dramatic rhythm as he follows the tension of extended verbal discourse with a swift burst of stage action that moves the plot in a shocking and unexpected direction.

While Leontes' denunciation of the oracle is predictable, his subsequent change of heart is a complete surprise. His jealousy vanishes as suddenly as it arose, almost as if he has been in a temporary state of demonic possession. Perhaps aware that such a sudden reversal might seem ludicrous, Shakespeare cleverly distracts attention from it by placing Hermione's swooning and removal at exactly this point; by the time she has been taken offstage, we are somehow more prepared to accept Leontes' public speech of apology, confession and repentance at face value.

The scene's final shock is still to come, however, with the entrance of Paulina and her revelation of Hermione's death — a revelation that she delays until the end of a 28-line speech of passionate recrimination to Leontes for his previous actions. This is a powerful piece of rhetoric, quite different in tone from Hermione's speeches earlier in the scene. Paulina is bitter, accusing, sarcastic, insulting and deeply emotional. However, in a striking change from his previous attitude to her 'boundless tongue' (II.3.91), Leontes now tells her, 'Thou canst not speak too much' (line 213). Her risky rhetoric has proved the genuineness of his guilty sorrow, which was presumably part of her intention, and it is left to the Lord to rebuke her for overstepping the mark.

Leontes' closing speech is the clearest and simplest he has uttered so far in the play and, like him, we anticipate a long and painful process in which the daily 'recreation', or pastime, of visiting the bodies of his wife and son, will lead to his moral and spiritual re-creation. Reflecting from the vantage point of the play's conclusion, we never think to ask what Paulina was going to show Leontes as she led him off to view the bodies; this is, after all, a fairy tale.

Pause for *Thought* ❙❙

This turning point is often marked in productions of the play by the beginning of a violent storm that continues into the scene of Antigonus's arrival in Bohemia. What effect do you think this creates, and is it necessary?

Pause for *Thought* ❙❙

How do you respond to the operation of justice in this scene? Is the term called into question?

Act III scene 3

Antigonus has landed on the stormy Bohemian coast, where he has decided to leave the baby, following a dream in which Hermione told him to do so. Naming the child 'Perdita' — the lost one — on Hermione's ghostly instructions, he interprets his dream as confirmation of her guilt and Polixenes' paternity. Placing the baby on the ground with a box and papers, he flees from a pursuing bear as the storm worsens. A Shepherd in search of two missing sheep finds the child, and his son enters to report the simultaneous sinking of the ship and killing of Antigonus by the bear. Opening the box, they discover gold. As he leaves with the child, his son goes off to bury Antigonus's remains.

Commentary: **Storms in Shakespeare are often symbolic of social and political disturbance, violence and bloodshed, while ghostly dreams and visions mark a moment of personal crisis for the characters who experience them. Both of these emblematic modes operate in the opening section of this scene. The abandonment of Perdita is not merely a pitiful human tragedy; it leaves the Sicilian throne without an heir, a situation that could lead, as Shakespeare's Jacobean audience knew only too well, to political instability and factionalism. On the individual level, however, it is a moral crime, and Antigonus and the mariners are punished by death for their complicity in it.**

The conclusion Antigonus draws from his dream is that if Hermione is dead she must have been executed after having been proved guilty of adultery by the oracle. This provides him with a convenient explanation for the ghost's choice of Bohemia as a suitable place to leave the baby, but it also, disconcertingly, undermines his hitherto unshakeable faith in Hermione's innocence.

The death of Antigonus, marked by that most famous of all Shakespearean stage directions, *'Exit, pursued by a bear'*, is the play's fulcrum, marking its change of mode from tragedy to comedy. The moment itself, though, has proved controversial. Is the bear's appearance in itself comic, or should the laughter begin only with the arrival of the Shepherd? We have no way of knowing Shakespeare's intentions, nor how the bear was presented in the first productions at the Globe or the Blackfriars. Modern stagings have taken a variety of decisions, with bears ranging from the ludicrous to the terrifying, from the symbolic to the realistic, from the solidly visible to the eerily suggestive.

Context

Belief about ghosts was inconsistent in Shakespeare's time: to some they represented the genuine spirits of the dead; for others they were false apparitions adopted by evil spirits to entice the unwary into damnation. Antigonus interprets his dream as a genuine visitation from the ghost of Hermione, who must therefore be dead since apparitions of the living were rare and usually deemed impossible. It seems, then, that Shakespeare wants to reinforce the audience's belief in Hermione's death.

Task 3

Consider and discuss the dramatic effect of different ways in which the bear might be represented on stage.

What is not in doubt is the relaxation into comedy with the arrival of the Shepherd; the transformation from courtly drama to rustic humour is reflected in the linguistic shift from blank verse to colloquial prose. Shakespeare does not patronise this Shepherd as a rustic stereotype, however; his humour derives from his knowing, worldly-wise commentary on contemporary life, from the indolence and irresponsibility of the young to the consequences of illicit sexual relations. His reaction on discovering the baby Perdita is down to earth and compassionate, but not sentimental.

His son, however, is a different matter. His account of the shipwreck and the death of Antigonus, which switches between events in his eagerness to describe both, transforms tragedy into comedy. It avoids being distasteful, however, through the sense of awe and wonder, mingled with simple compassion, that underlies the excited confusion of the language.

Pause for _Thought_ ❚❚

Do you feel that this scene provides an effective bridge between the worlds of tragedy and comedy?

Top ten **_quotation_**⟩

There is considerable scope for the actors to develop the comedy of this scene, yet it should always remain rooted in the characters as defined by the words they speak. Having found wealth, there is real comic potential in the Shepherd's sudden abandonment of the prize sheep he had been so eager to find: 'Let my sheep go' (line 110). This is gentle, character-based comedy and, as a result, Shakespeare is able to retain an essential thematic seriousness, granting the Shepherd what many critics see as one of the play's key symbolic lines, 'Thou met'st with things dying, I with things new born' (lines 100–1). Modern productions almost invariably take their interval at the close of this scene.

(See also Sample Essay 1 on the free website at www.philipallan. co.uk/literatureguidesonline which analyses the Shepherd's first speech.)

Act IV scene 1

Time moves us on 16 years, and tells us of Leontes' self-imposed confinement. He speaks of Perdita having grown up as the Shepherd's daughter, and mentions Polixenes' son, whom he now names as Florizel.

Commentary: **In Shakespeare's use of Time to begin the play's second movement a number of traditions of early modern drama come together. As the personification of an abstract concept, he is a reminder of the old morality plays in which such 'characters'** enacted the moral and spiritual dilemmas of human existence. Time embodies a thematic concept, making us aware not only of the temporal context of human existence, but suggesting that time is needed for wounds to heal and the great cycles of birth, death and regeneration to take their course. In his morality guise, Time was presumably presented on stage with his traditional accoutrements of white beard, scythe, wings and hourglass — the last two of which he refers to in his speech. Time's thematic control of the play is indicated in two small touches, which are easily overlooked. When he says, 'remember well/I mentioned a son o'th'king's' (line 22), he is taking upon himself the role of dramatist, since Time, of course, has not previously appeared in the play, and we learned of Polixenes' son through the dialogue of Act I scene 2. Furthermore, in referring to 'that wide gap' (line 7), he is anticipating the play's closing speech, in which Leontes, too, refers to the 'wide gap of time' covered by the events of the play.

Time's function is also that of chorus, a dramatic device which originated in Greek tragedy as a group of actors whose communal speaking provided a commentary on the events of the play. In Elizabethan and Jacobean theatre, however, the chorus was normally a single actor whose role combined such commentary with linking narration and the establishment of a direct relationship with the audience, as well as frequently providing a prologue and/or epilogue.

In concluding his speech by hoping the audience members are enjoying themselves, Time is employing the kind of false modesty in drawing attention to the play as theatrical performance that was a familiar part of other Shakespearean choruses.

Another tradition of Greek drama, outlined in Aristotle's *Poetics*, is the concept of the unities of Time, Place and Action, and Shakespeare blatantly draws attention to his complete disregard of these dramatic 'rules' by having Time ask us to 'Impute it not a crime/...that I slide/O'er sixteen years' (lines 4–7).

To mark out Time's role as both chorus and allegorical morality figure, Shakespeare employs rhyming couplets — the only use of rhyme in the play except for the lyrics of the songs. Together with the rather awkwardly structured, archaic language, this creates the effect of an old-fashioned character, appropriate to Old Father Time, and lends a slightly comic edge to his

Context

Shakespeare often used the chorus device, notably in *Henry V*, where the chorus is arguably the second most important character in the play, and later in *Pericles*, where the medieval poet Gower provides a running commentary on the events of the drama.

Pause for **Thought** 🕚

What do you feel are the most important dramatic functions of Time? Could the character have been dispensed with?

appearance. In the modern theatre, his role offers a challenge, and directors have presented him in a variety of ingenious ways, including as the traditional figure of an old man with an hourglass, as a child, as a golden bird, and as Shakespeare himself.

Act IV scene 2

Polixenes tries to persuade Camillo not to return to Sicilia, though Leontes has sent for him. He changes the subject to Prince Florizel's increasingly regular absences from court, and reveals that his spies have observed him visiting the home of a Shepherd who has an attractive daughter and who has grown mysteriously wealthy. They decide to visit the Shepherd's house in disguise to discover the reason for Florizel's visits.

Commentary: **Short scenes with apparently little dramatic interest can often be rewarding to examine closely. In terms of the play's structure and the development of its story, we need to be reintroduced to Polixenes and Camillo at this point, and to learn the state of affairs in Bohemia. The scene raises immediate questions, however. Why does Shakespeare give no visible indication of the life of Polixenes' court — no lords or servants, such as those surrounding Leontes in Acts I–III; no Archidamus, whom we met at the start of the play? In addition, why do this king and his most trusted counsellor speak in prose rather than the verse one might expect? A prose, moreover, that is flat and colourless, lacking both the exaggerated artificiality that gives energy to Camillo's and Archidamus's dialogue in Act I scene 1, and the colloquial vigour that enlivens the speech of Autolycus and the rustic characters.**

Part of the explanation perhaps lies in the fact that we are seeing the end of a conversation — one in which Camillo has been 'importunate' in his requests to be allowed to visit Sicilia but is now forced to give up hope. There is a certain life in some of the antithetical, balanced sentences, such as Polixenes' continuation of the play's disease imagery, ''Tis a sickness denying thee anything; a death to grant this' (lines 1–2). As the scene turns into little more than a sharing of information about Florizel, however, so the style becomes dully factual: 'it is three days since I saw the prince' (line 23); 'he is seldom from the house of a most homely shepherd' (lines 29–30). There is very little

of the richness of imagery found elsewhere in the play: Perdita is 'of most rare note' and 'the angle that plucks' Florizel to the Shepherd's cottage; otherwise the situation is explained with surprising literalness.

We are, however, given something of an insight into the workings of Polixenes' court, even though, perhaps because all available actors are preparing themselves for the sheep-shearing scene, we never see it in action. It appears that even Camillo is not fully aware of the extent of the king's intelligence service, of which he has to be told. 'I have eyes under my service…from whom I have this intelligence' (lines 28–29), Polixenes informs him. How are we meant to respond to a king who has his own son spied on? Perhaps this merely goes with his selfishness in denying Camillo's request to return to Sicilia, which can only be excused by the lingering effects of his experience there 16 years previously.

However, Polixenes' dwelling on the past and the intriguing undercurrents of courtly espionage are not enough to give much dramatic life to the scene, which is lacking in real tension or conflict, its main purpose being to bring us up to date briskly and prepare us for future developments. Shakespeare, however, knows his craft. By making the opening of the second part of the play so flat and undramatic, he is simply enhancing the impact of Autolycus's vivid eruption into the action, and the vigour and energy of all that follows.

Act IV scene 3

Autolycus enters singing, and introduces himself as a rogue and former courtier, who once served Prince Florizel. Pretending to be the victim of robbery, he picks the pockets of the Clown, who is on his way to buy provisions for his sister for the sheep-shearing feast, at which Autolycus tells us he will be present.

Commentary: **The entrance of Autolycus into the play represents a crucial turning point in its mood and action. He enters singing, and it is through his songs and the impressions they create that he makes his initial impact. The songs are lively and energetic, projecting a cheerfully amoral attitude to life, telling of unrepentant thieving against a natural background of spring flowers and birdsong: 'When daffodils begin to peer' (line 1); 'With heigh the sweet birds, O how they sing!' (line 6). Autolycus**

*Pause for **Thought***

How do you respond to the idea that Shakespeare did not always write brilliantly?

*Task **4***

Compare this scene with Act I scene 1. What are the most significant similarities and differences? You could make a chart to set out your ideas.

leaves the scene as he entered it, with a song praising the virtues of the outdoor life and 'a merry heart'.

Between his snatches of song, Autolycus addresses the audience directly, not in traditional soliloquy, but in the beguiling, button-holing manner of a stand-up comic. In less than ten lines, he gives us information about his name, his recent history ('I have served Prince Florizel…but now I am out of service', lines 13–14); his current occupation ('My traffic is sheets' (line 23), 'a snapper-up of unconsidered trifles', line 25); the source of his clothes ('with die and drab I purchased this caparison', lines 25–26); and his attitude to a life in which the fear of 'Gallows and knock…Beating and hanging' (lines 27–28), causes him to 'sleep out' all thoughts of 'the life to come'. Shakespeare's exposition here is nothing if not economical.

The relationship Autolycus thus creates with the audience is crucial in our developing response to him. It enables him to share asides with us while conning the Clown, partly implicating us in his actions. When he returns to addressing the audience directly after the Clown's exit, he can tell us what he intends to do next, planting in our minds the expectation of seeing him in action again at the sheep-shearing.

Stage action is in fact one of the principal devices Shakespeare uses to present Autolycus. In this scene we have no sooner discovered how he makes his living than we see him practising his skills on the hapless Clown. The humour of the episode is linguistic as much as physical, however, with Autolycus's exaggerated politeness ('sweet sir', 'good-faced sir'); his relish of the portrait he paints of his own character, in the guise of describing his attacker; and the comically ironic double meanings implicit in statements such as 'Offer me no money,/I pray you' (lines 71–72), thus avoiding the Clown's finding out that he no longer has any, and 'he, sir, he: that's the rogue that put me into this apparel' (lines 90–91) — a statement that is no more than the truth.

Shakespeare also characterises Autolycus through the quality of his colloquial prose speech. He is eloquent and articulate, with a powerful command of rhetorical devices such as balanced, often antithetical sentences. His wit frequently emerges in vivid metaphorical language and wordplay, as in 'Your purse is not hot enough to purchase your spice' (lines 103–04), or 'If the springe hold, the cock's mine' (line 32). Yet his vocabulary is rooted in everyday life, with talk of sheets, bailiffs, tinkers, puppet shows and bear-baitings. The imagery of his songs, however, lifts our appreciation of his character to another level. Though still harping on the ordinary life of 'the doxy' or the enjoyment of 'a quart of ale', the vocabulary of the songs is set against the evocation of a rural landscape of birds and flowers, haystacks and moonlit nights, footpaths and stiles.

While this language prepares us for the subsequent pastoral scenes, Shakespeare also invites us to consider a more symbolic function for this new character who, in a play entitled *The Winter's Tale*, sings of 'summer songs' and asserts that 'the red blood reigns in the winter's pale'. The positive associations of 'red blood' may remind us of Paulina's 'red-looked anger' (II.2.34) and anticipate Florizel's injunction, 'let's be red with mirth' (IV.4.54). 'Pale' may suggest the constricting boundaries of the moral kingdoms over which Leontes and Polixenes 'reign', the one destroyed by his own jealousy, the other last seen planning to spy further on the activities of his son. In the play's imaginative world, these wintry realms are now usurped by the life-enhancing spirit of Autolycus's eruption into the action.

'Pale' may suggest...the moral kingdoms over which Leontes and Polixenes 'reign'

...these wintry realms are now usurped by the life-enhancing spirit of Autolycus's eruption into the action

Act IV scene 4

Florizel and Perdita discuss their love for each another. She, dressed as queen of the feast, is apprehensive about the consequences of their relationship; he, disguised as a shepherd, Doricles, is more confident. The Shepherd enters with the Clown, the disguised Polixenes and Camillo, and all the other guests. Perdita welcomes the visitors and gives them flowers, engaging with Polixenes in a discussion on the art of grafting. Polixenes and Camillo note something about her that lifts her above her station in life, and during the dance that follows, Polixenes asks the Shepherd about Florizel. The Shepherd gives his opinion that the young couple love each other equally.

The Shepherd's servant announces the arrival of a pedlar and ballad-monger, who turns out to be the disguised Autolycus. Mopsa and Dorcas, who are rivals for the Clown's affections, join Autolycus in the singing of a ballad appropriate to their situation.

After the dance, Polixenes engages Florizel in conversation about his feelings towards Perdita and pushes him into a declaration of his love for her. Perdita echoes his feelings and the Shepherd expresses approval of their match, but Polixenes argues that Florizel's father should be

Autolycus at the sheep-shearing feast, from a production at the Watermill Theatre, Newbury, in 2005

consulted, drawing an irritable response from the prince. Polixenes reveals his true identity and issues a series of angry threats: he will disinherit his son and subject Perdita to torture and death if they continue to see each other, while the Shepherd, first threatened with death, will suffer only the king's displeasure. On Polixenes' departure, the anguished lovers assess the situation. Seeing an opportunity to fulfil his own wish to return to Sicilia, Camillo suggests that they should visit Leontes there, on the pretext of a diplomatic mission, while he tries to talk Polixenes into accepting their union.

While Florizel discusses practicalities with Camillo, Autolycus returns, gloating over the profit he has made, not only from the sale of his trinkets but from his pickpocketing exploits. Camillo gives Autolycus money to change clothes with Florizel, while Perdita is to wear Florizel's hat, so that they can reach the ship undetected. Camillo's intention is to tell the king where the lovers have fled, so that, accompanying him in his pursuit of them, he will be able to return to Sicilia. Autolycus accosts the Shepherd and Clown, who are anxiously debating the wisdom of telling the king the truth about Perdita's origins. Removing his false beard and pretending to be a courtier, Autolycus interrogates them, tells them they cannot see the king at the palace because he has gone on board his new ship, and terrifies them with the prospect of the dreadful tortures that lie in store for them, while pretending not to know who they are. He agrees, though, to escort them to the king, for which they pay him gold. In reality, Autolycus intends to take them to Florizel's ship, hoping for further rewards from the prince.

Commentary: **This long scene is structured essentially as a sequential narrative. Shakespeare begins by introducing us to** the final pair of new characters, Florizel and Perdita, whose relationship is central to the remainder of the play. From the start of the scene, there is a clear contrast in their characters and their attitudes to their situation. Both are dressed up in costumes that reverse their social status: Perdita as queen of the feast, Florizel as a shepherd. Florizel revels in these transformations, suggesting that her 'unusual weeds...give a life' to each part of her (lines 1–2), and equating himself with those gods who transformed themselves into lesser creatures — bull, ram and 'poor humble swain' — for the sake of love. Perdita, though, is uneasy about her dressing up and his disguise: he is 'obscured/With a swain's wearing' (lines 8–9) and she 'most goddess-like pranked up' (line 10).

Perdita's discomfort is closely bound up with her intense awareness of the difference in status between herself and Florizel which, as she says, 'forges dread'. This is a strong word, but her fear is palpable as she confesses, 'I tremble/To think your father.../Should pass this way' (lines 18–20). Florizel's response to her concerns is confident and even dismissive, with a complacency that is not particularly attractive in its apparent absence of sympathetic understanding. All he can do is offer a series of instructions to her, expressed in the imperative: 'Apprehend nothing but jollity', 'darken not/The mirth o'th'feast', 'Be merry', 'Strangle such thoughts as these', 'Lift up your countenance', 'Address yourself to entertain them sprightly.' Although in these commands he is in tune with the celebratory atmosphere of this section of the play, concluding 'let's be red with mirth' (line 54), his insistence suggests a shallow understanding of the reality of their situation. However, his evident love for Perdita is strongly expressed, and he impressively distances himself from accusations of merely physical infatuation through the strength of his comment, 'my desires/Run not before mine honour, nor my lusts/Burn hotter than my faith' (lines 33–35).

Perdita's unwillingness to play a role is made evident in her initial reluctance to enter into the spirit of the festivities. She remains aware of the power of acting to reshape reality, as is made clear by her comment:

> Methinks I play as I have seen them do
> In Whitsun pastorals; sure this robe of mine
> Does change my disposition.   (lines 133–35)

❮ Top ten *quotation*

Unease about acting and performance was widespread in Shakespeare's time. Without an important patron (King James at this point in the life of Shakespeare's company) actors were regarded as rogues and vagabonds. Pretending to be someone else was seen as morally dubious.

When circumstances change, she is only too eager to discard what she sees as her artificial self: 'I'll queen it no inch farther' (line 428); she remains reluctant to adopt disguises, even out of necessity, later in the scene, when she says, 'I see the play so lies/That I must bear a part' (lines 624–25). Sensing her unease, Camillo firmly responds, 'No remedy.'

It is in her distribution of flowers to the assembled company that Perdita's role in the scene reaches its height. Combining the flower imagery itself with references to the seasons, her language embodies some of the play's central issues, with the inexorable cycle of life seen symbolically under the control of 'great creating nature'. To modern sensibilities, these flower speeches may seem to make her romantically sentimental, but looked at more closely the language is often expressive of strength and power, as with the daffodils that 'come before the swallow dares, and take/The winds of March with beauty' (lines 119–20). 'Take' literally means to enchant — itself a much stronger verb in Shakespeare's time than it has since become, suggestive of a hypnotic magical power. It also implies that the daffodils vigorously enjoy the wind's strength, or even take control of it, and the verb has sexual connotations too. The daffodils here are not the sentimentalised flowers of modern greetings card verses, but vibrant and vigorous manifestations of natural beauty — more courageous than the swallow, suggests Perdita, in braving the boisterous March winds. Such qualities thus attach themselves to Perdita too, when the winds of Polixenes' wrath fail to shake her determination:

> I was not much afeard, for once or twice
> I was about to speak and tell him plainly
> The self-same sun that shines upon his court
> Hides not his visage from our cottage but
> Looks on alike.   (lines 421–425)

In these lines, she seems to be promoting a kind of humane social equality, despite her earlier unhappiness with the difference in status between herself and Florizel; her moral courage continues when she later asserts, 'I think affliction may subdue the cheek,/But not take in the mind' (lines 555–56). Yet Perdita does not actually respond in the face of Polixenes' angry threats, and she is largely silent during the remainder of the scene, speaking fewer than ten lines out of the 218 that remain before she, Florizel and Camillo exit. It is almost as if

Shakespeare reduces her status to the feminine stereotype of silent victimhood, emphasised by her determination to 'milk [her] ewes, and weep'.

Central to our impression of Perdita in this scene is her debate with Polixenes on the subject of grafting, in which the relative merits of 'art' and 'nature' are held up for examination. Perdita objects to growing 'carnations' and 'gillyvors' because they are not natural, but the artificial products of grafting and cross-breeding. Polixenes argues that all such activities are natural, because the humans who carry them out are themselves part of nature, so that 'over that art,/Which...adds to nature, is an art/ That nature makes' (lines 90–92) — thus, 'the art itself is nature' (line 97). Perdita is forced to admit he is right — 'so it is' — but stubbornly refuses to change her initial conviction.

The debate is deepened for the audience by the various levels of irony that underlie it, in which the two debaters essentially argue for a position on the issue of grafting which is opposite to that they adopt on the level of personal and social relationships. Polixenes may advocate that a gardener should 'marry/A gentler scion to the wildest stock,/[To] make conceive a bark of baser kind/By bud of nobler race' (lines 92–95), but will not countenance such interbreeding in the case of his son and a shepherdess. Perdita, conversely, objects to such interbreeding in botany, but is herself engaged in it at the human level. The complex irony is deepened by the audience's awareness that she is not in fact a shepherdess at all, but a princess, and that Polixenes' true 'nature' is concealed by the 'art' of disguise.

Florizel also demonstrates a mixture of attractive and unattractive qualities. He expresses his love for Perdita in beautiful and lyrical language when he addresses her directly, notably in his speech beginning, 'What you do/Still betters what is done' (lines 135–36), its rhythms and onomatopoeic effects gently reflecting the 'wave o'th'sea' to which he likens her; and with forceful sincerity when he is pushed by Polixenes into a public defence of his feelings for her, asserting that he 'would not prize' any worldly accomplishments 'without her love'. Yet he can also seem pompous, self-righteous and arrogant, particularly in his discussion with the 'ancient sir' whom he fails to recognise as his father, whose views he dismisses with what can be seen as discourteous contempt:

*Pause for **Thought***

Is Perdita largely presented here as a forthright, confident young woman or as a passive victim of male authority? Note this view of her character: 'Shakespeare blends the realistic and the symbolic with the surest touch. ...Perdita...is one of Shakespeare's richest characters; at once a symbol and a human being' (E. M. W. Tillyard, *Shakespeare's Last Plays*, 1938).

I yield all this;
But for some other reasons, my grave sir,
Which 'tis not fit you know, I not acquaint
My father of this business.   (lines 389–92)

There is something callous, too, in his reference to his father's
prospective death: 'One being dead,/I shall have more than you
can dream of yet' (lines 366–67).

Florizel comes across much more sympathetically in his
conversation with Camillo after the king's departure. His
language is infused with love, sincerity and strength of purpose,
and while his own plans are rash and impulsive, he submits
himself with respect and sensitivity to Camillo's guidance.

Polixenes and Camillo arouse mixed responses in the scene.
Their impact also depends on the kind of disguises they are
given which, in some productions, can make them seem rather
comic at first. At the start, Polixenes seems reasonable, and
he is impressed by Perdita's poise and beauty, as is Camillo,
recognising that 'Nothing she does or seems/But smacks of
something greater than herself,/Too noble for this place' (lines
157–59). He gives ample opportunity for Florizel to take a
different course of action in pursuing his love, but his apparent
reasonableness is shattered by the violence of his anger and
the cruelty of his threats when he reveals his true identity. It is
instructive to compare his role here with that of Leontes in the
first part of the play; if he seems a less powerful character, this
simply reflects the different nature of his passionate feelings and
the different context in which they are displayed. As the father
furious with his child's independence in choosing relationships,
Polixenes is partly a familiar stereotype that runs through
Shakespeare's drama from Egeus in *A Midsummer Night's Dream*
and Capulet in *Romeo and Juliet* to the king in *Cymbeline*.

Camillo, meanwhile, is a more transparent character, amusingly
so in his admiration of Perdita, with whom he flirts wittily in
his comment, 'I should leave grazing, were I of your flock,/
And only live by gazing' (lines 109–10). He retains his disguise
after Polixenes has revealed himself, and his remaining behind
when his master sweeps out suggests a certain disapproval
of the king's behaviour, similar to his response to Leontes'
jealousy in Act I. There are selfish reasons, however, behind
Camillo's helping of the lovers, and there is a sense in which
he underplays the dangers and uncertainties of the course he

Pause for **Thought**

Do you feel this
scene is dramatically
effective, or too long
for its purpose?

advises — a course that achieves his desire to revisit Sicilia. He shares this with the audience in two clumsy asides as Florizel and Perdita talk apart (lines 486–92 and 631–36). Camillo should nevertheless remain an honest character, motivated largely by loyalty and sympathy, and it is clear that he will pursue his own ends only in the context of working towards the reconciliation of Polixenes and Florizel, and promoting the union of the prince and Perdita. In imagery typical of the play, Florizel appropriately calls him 'the medicine of our house' (line 566).

Act V scene 1

The action returns to Sicilia, where Cleomenes and Dion attempt to persuade Leontes that he has performed more than ample penance for his sins, and urge him to consider remarriage in order to provide the kingdom with an heir. Paulina opposes them, however, and Leontes promises not to take a new wife without her permission — which she says she will only give when Hermione is restored to life. A servant announces the unexpected arrival of Florizel and his princess, and Leontes welcomes the visitors, in whom he sees the image of his lost son and daughter. Florizel offers greetings from Polixenes, and claims that Perdita is a Libyan princess whom he has married. A lord announces Polixenes' arrival in Sicilia with the revelation that Perdita is a mere shepherd's daughter, and that she and Florizel should be apprehended. The Shepherd and Clown have also arrived in Sicilia, and Polixenes has threatened to torture them to death. Florizel assumes he and Perdita have been betrayed by Camillo, who is with Polixenes, and confesses that they are not married. Leontes, expressing admiration for Perdita's beauty despite her lowly status, agrees to act as an advocate for the young lovers with Polixenes.

Commentary: **Shakespeare's first concern in this scene is to show the changes that have taken place in Leontes since the start of the play. Sixteen years of penance have transformed him from a volatile, unstable tyrant, subject to paranoid delusions, into a calm, reflective recluse, unable to forget the wife and children destroyed by his own intemperate actions. These changes are made explicit in every aspect of his language, from the evenness of its verse rhythms to the clarity of its grammatical structures and the quality of its imagery. He is entirely under the influence of Paulina who, with her usual sharpness, takes every opportunity to remind him of what he has destroyed.**

Taking it **Further** ▶

In 2001 Nicholas Hytner staged Act IV scene 4 along the lines of Glastonbury festival; Matthew Warchus in 2002 gave it the feel of Rodgers and Hammerstein's *Oklahoma*. Research these two productions and their staging of this scene and discuss which you prefer.

Leontes' inertia and Paulina's controlling influence are creating increasingly urgent political anxieties for his lords, centred on the absence of an heir to the throne.

We are prepared for Florizel and Perdita's unexpected arrival by the enthusiastic speech of the servant, in which Perdita's qualities are significantly linked to those of Hermione. Florizel and Perdita have been engaged in a serious deception since their first appearance in the play, but their status as romantic lovers has somehow justified their behaviour, which in any case seems to be a purely domestic affair. In fact, Florizel's determination to marry a shepherd's daughter would have severe political repercussions for the kingdom of Bohemia, particularly if Polixenes stuck to his threat to 'bar [Florizel] from succession' (IV.4.408), plunging the country into a crisis similar to that facing Sicilia.

In this final part of the scene, Leontes himself acquires a genuine air of decisive authority — probably the first and only time in the play where we see him behaving as a king ideally should. Yet his role here, and indeed earlier in the scene, is undercut by some rather dubious remarks that impart an edgy quality to the proceedings. His response to Perdita, for example, is somewhat ambiguous. Like the servant, he is struck by her beauty and calls her 'goddess' and 'paragon', and it is clear that she makes him think of both his wife and his own lost daughter: twice he imagines that in looking at Florizel and Perdita he might be looking at his own children (lines 131–33, 175–77). On learning that Perdita is no more than a shepherdess, his reaction is conventional: he is sorry she is 'not so rich in worth as beauty' (line 213), as if 'worth' were a quality defined purely by social status. Almost immediately, however, he finds himself thinking of her in another way, as a potential wife for himself. If, as Florizel says, Polixenes would grant him anything, he would 'beg [Florizel's] precious mistress' (line 222). To the knowing audience, this has unfortunate suggestions of incest — something more explicitly developed in Greene's *Pandosto* (see 'Sources of the play' on pp. 69–70 of this guide). He answers Paulina's rebuke, however, by explaining that his comment was motivated solely by Perdita's resemblance to his wife.

The imagery of the scene is partly responsible for creating its particular atmosphere of serenity and acceptance tinged with enduring sadness and regret. Cleomenes sets the tone with the religious vocabulary of his opening speech, expressed in the Christian terminology of sin, penance and redemption. Only his reference to 'the heavens' rather than 'Heaven' reminds us that the play's action ostensibly moves in a setting of pagan theology. Leontes, too, uses similar vocabulary, in one speech referring to Polixenes as 'holy', 'graceful', 'sacred' and 'blest', regretting the 'sin' he has committed against him, and invoking both 'the blessèd gods' and 'the heavens'. In welcoming the young lovers, Leontes also employs two of the play's other key images — the seasons and disease. In each case he sees their arrival as the opportunity for a new beginning: they come 'as...the spring to th'earth' (line 151), and he hopes that the gods will 'purge all infection' from the air during their stay (line 168).

...the young lovers...come 'as...the spring to th'earth'

Act V scene 2

Autolycus learns, through the discussion of three Gentlemen, of the reunion of Leontes with Polixenes and Camillo, and the revelation of Perdita's true identity. Paulina has invited the assembled company to view the statue of Hermione that she has had made. Autolycus reflects ruefully on his unknowing role in bringing about these remarkable events. The Shepherd and Clown, revelling in their new status as gentlemen, promise to put in a good word to Florizel on Autolycus's behalf, providing he mends his ways.

Commentary: **If we do not know the story, we are likely to expect the play to conclude with the reunion of the two kings and the revelation that Perdita is Leontes' lost daughter. It comes as an enormous surprise, then, to find these events recounted at second hand by three brand new characters. Only when we learn of Hermione's statue does it become clear that Shakespeare has another conclusion planned: one which, despite the hints he supplies, we have little chance of predicting.**

We have not heard language quite the same as the Gentlemen's courtly, artificial prose since the play's opening dialogue between Camillo and Archidamus. Its effect here is difficult to judge, and its impact on stage is often rather undramatic. There is no doubt that it is partly intended to be comic, as if the speakers are vying with each other to see who can provide the most rhetorically impressive account. Certainly, the many rhetorical devices in these speeches seem self-consciously elaborate. The persistent antithetical balance is notable, in

Pause for **Thought**

Consider the critic Mark Van Doren's view of the scene: 'Shakespeare disappoints our expectation in one important respect. The recognition of Leontes and his daughter takes place off stage; we only hear three gentlemen talking prose about it...., and are denied the satisfaction of such a scene as we might have supposed would crown the play'. (1939)

phrases that oppose 'speech' with 'dumbness', 'language' with 'gesture' and, on three separate occasions, 'joy' with 'sorrow', as well as highlighting contrasting verbs: 'ransomed'/'destroyed'; 'seen'/'spoken of'; 'lost'/'found'; and 'declined'/'elevated'.

Other rhetorical devices are employed too, most commonly by the Third Gentleman, to whom the bulk of the account belongs. He employs the listing technique in the 'proofs' of Perdita's identity, and self-consciously points up his own witty use of metaphor in remarking that Perdita's emotional response was the sight that 'angled for [his] eyes — caught the water though not the fish' (line 66).

Top ten **quotation** 〉

Ballads have featured earlier in the play, often dealing with grotesque and impossible occurrences, but this event, according to the Second Gentleman, was so amazing 'that ballad-makers cannot be able to express it' (line 20). It is, in fact, more like 'an old tale', as both Second and Third Gentlemen describe it: something that has to be told 'though credit be asleep and not an ear open' (line 50) — in other words, even though no one is likely to believe it. Perhaps the play too, as a winter's tale, is meant to be seen in this way. Yet there are more serious matters involved, such as the suggestion that 'all the instruments which aided to expose the child were even then lost when it was found' (lines 56–57), thus investing the deaths of Antigonus and the sailors with a sense of moral retribution. Furthermore, there is a touching description of Leontes' moral courage in recounting to Perdita the circumstances of her mother's death: 'with the manner how she came to't bravely confessed and lamented by the king' (lines 67–68). All this would have been dramatic material for a direct enactment of the scene, but perhaps Shakespeare thought it would detract from the impact of the surprise denouement he had planned.

*Pause for **Thought*** ⏸

The Clown and the Shepherd, despite what they say to Autolycus, are not specified in the stage directions as being present when the queen's statue is unveiled. Would you include them on stage in the final scene?

Shakespeare has a further purpose in this scene, namely to conclude the roles of Autolycus, the Shepherd and the Clown. Autolycus, who entered the play with such a dramatic flourish, leaves it with a distinct whimper. Not only is he denied any concluding songs, but he is sidelined by the Gentlemen's discussion and bested by his former victims, whose assistance he has to beg in restoring him to favour with Florizel. The old Autolycus would certainly be an inappropriate presence in the subdued atmosphere of the play's conclusion, but the fading out of his role is a definite anticlimax. It is satisfying, though, that the rustics have the upper hand, and the comedy of their naïve response to their social elevation is not without a certain dignity. It is notable that Autolycus's four responses to the Clown are brief and subservient, and he is not even allowed the last word. It is as if, uprooted from his native environment, there is no role for him in the world of Sicilia.

Act V scene 3

Paulina reveals the statue of Hermione to her assembled guests. They wonder at its life-like quality, and are powerfully moved by the feelings and memories it evokes. Paulina claims to be able to make the statue move and, as it comes to life to the sound of music, it is revealed to be the real Hermione, preserved alive with Paulina's aid in the hope that her lost daughter would one day be found. She embraces Leontes and gives Perdita her blessing. Paulina wryly acknowledges her exclusion from this reunion, since her own husband cannot be restored to her, but Leontes pairs her off with Camillo, offers a final plea to Hermione and Polixenes to forgive his jealous suspicions, and urges Paulina to lead the company away to share each other's stories.

Commentary: **The final scene of *The Winter's Tale* never fails to exert a powerful and moving effect, even in an otherwise indifferent production. In the modern theatre, even when we do not know the story, we are likely to guess the outcome as soon as we see the statue revealed, since it is usually clear that it is, in fact, the actor who played Hermione. Jacobean audiences, however, would be used to seeing statues represented on stage by real actors — presumably this saved on the expense of creating elaborate props. Thus it would be a genuine surprise when the 'statue' moved. Yet the scene does not rely on this element of surprise in creating its magical effect; after all, many of those first audiences must have revealed the ending to friends who were going to**

Task 5

Imagine that Autolycus and the Clown and Shepherd have been present at or have heard about the concluding moments of the play. Write their different accounts of those events. Bring out the likely differences in their points of view.

Paulina unveils the 'statue', in the Royal Shakespeare Company production of 2009

Donald Cooper/Rex Features

see the play, and it must have been familiar to spectators at the numerous court performances given between 1611 and 1640. So how does Shakespeare ensure that, whether we know the outcome or not, the denouement retains its sense of mystery and wonder?

The key to the scene's effect lies mostly in the careful use of Paulina as both director and stage manager. First she builds up her visitors' anticipation by giving them a tour of the rest of her gallery before revealing the statue. She cunningly calculates its effect on them, twice warning them not to touch it because the paint is still wet (lines 47 and 81–82), threatening three times to close the curtain because of the powerful emotional effect it has produced (lines 59, 68 and 83), and persistently hinting at the possibility that the statue might move and even come to life (lines 60–61, 69–70, 74–75 and 87–89). This piece of carefully staged theatre then reaches its climax accompanied by the dramatic use of music, as Paulina gently prompts the still Hermione into motion.

To a large extent, Shakespeare uses the reactions of Paulina's onstage spectators to guide the response of the real audience. Their sense of wonder and amazement rubs off on us, and her injunction to Leontes, 'It is required/You do awake your faith' (lines 94–95), acts also as an exhortation to us to suspend our disbelief.

When Paulina promises to make the statue move, she is anxious to 'protest against' the assumption that she is 'assisted/By wicked powers' (lines 90–91), and urges those who think she is engaged in 'unlawful business' to depart. As Hermione descends, Paulina reassures the company that 'her actions shall be holy as/You hear my spell is lawful' (lines 104–05). Leontes is not quite convinced: 'If this be magic,' he says, 'let it be an art/Lawful as eating' (lines 110–11).

Having descended from the pedestal, Hermione embraces Leontes but does not speak to him; after all, as many commentators have pointed out, what could she possibly say? Her only speech is addressed to her daughter, for whose sake, she makes it clear, she has 'preserved' herself and, using the same word, asks to hear how Perdita has been 'preserved'.

The precise degree of harmony and reconciliation embodied in the happy ending is, however much debated. It is already crafted to contain unresolved elements of tragedy, in the deaths of Mamillius, Antigonus and the mariners, which cannot be

Taking it
Further

Read Edwin Morgan's poem 'Instructions to an Actor' (pp. 198–200 of the Cambridge School Shakespeare edition of the play) and consider what it reveals about the dramatic impact of the statue scene.

redeemed by time. In Nicholas Hytner's 2001 National Theatre production, these elements were enhanced by a sense of awkwardness in the reunion of Leontes and Hermione, by the distinctly cool reaction of Paulina to Leontes' sudden proposal that she should marry Camillo, and by the concluding image of Hermione and Perdita, not having gone off with the others, 'clutching each other like shipwreck survivors' in the words of the reviewer Paul Taylor. Perhaps this is going too much against the grain of the text, but there is no doubting the ambiguities with which Shakespeare has invested the ending. Note the following two examples of different critical views:

> When Hermione descends from the pedestal into her husband's arms, the impossibility of reconciliation is passed by in silence, and Leontes busies himself in finding a husband for the aged and unattractive Paulina. (Robert Bridges, 1907)

> Hermione, then, comes back from the dead, and the hushed and gracious verse of the statue scene speaks of the resurrection of the Christian to eternal life here and hereafter.' (S. L. Bethell, 1956)

Many of the play's recurring images are rounded off in this scene. Paulina draws attention to the play's likeness to 'an old tale' which might be 'hooted at', yet hooting is the very last response that the scene evokes, suggesting that a 'winter's tale' may not necessarily be something trivial and laughable. The recurring processes of time and seasonal change are invoked again in Perdita's reference to the queen who 'ended when I but began' (line 45), and Camillo's description of Leontes' sorrow, 'Which sixteen winters cannot blow away,/So many summers dry' (lines 50–51). The 'statue' of Hermione arouses further consideration of the relationship between art and nature, representing both; and the art of the theatre, in particular, is suggested by the metatheatrical qualities of the whole scene, as staged by Paulina. Leontes himself is aware that, in the words of Jaques in *As You Like It*, 'all the world's a stage', when he ends the play by suggesting that each of them should 'answer to his part/Performed in this wide gap of time' (lines 153–54). A feeling of intense satisfaction is engendered in the audience by their knowledge that they have been privileged spectators of the events that the characters must now share with each other offstage.

*Pause for **Thought*** ⏸

How far do you feel that a sense of harmony and reconciliation is achieved in this final scene?

❮ Top ten *quotation*

Task **6**

Write the speeches given by Polixenes and Leontes at the wedding of Florizel and Perdita. You will have to decide whether to make these speeches significantly different in tone and content. Include some reference to past events and bring out important aspects of the kings' relationship to each other as well as to their children.

Themes

Responding to the themes of a complex drama such as *The Winter's Tale* is not as simple as asking what the 'moral' of the play is. The themes range across personal relationships, social structures, religious and political morality and philosophical reflections on the meaning of life; they are made evident through plot and narrative, characterisation, language and imagery.

Personal themes

Friendship and marriage

The first kind of relationship brought to our attention in the play is the friendship between Leontes and Polixenes, which began in their boyhood. In talking to Hermione, Polixenes stresses the innocence of their friendship, suggesting that this was in some way compromised by their subsequent relationships with women (I.2.76–80). Leontes, however, identifies Hermione's acceptance of his marriage proposal, after three months' delay, as equal in value to her success in persuading Polixenes to extend his visit to Sicilia (I.2.88–105). Marriage is thus balanced against friendship — two of the cornerstones of human relationships. Therefore, as Polixenes points out, when Leontes believes that he and Hermione have been engaged in an adulterous affair, his sense of betrayal must be exacerbated (I.2.451–57). The theme of betrayal is developed further in the behaviour of Camillo in both parts of the play.

Jealousy

Leontes' mistrust of his wife and friend is mistaken, however. His suspicions are motivated by inexplicable psychological disturbance and his jealousy becomes the key theme of the play's first movement. Its effects spread far beyond his circle of family and friends to have political repercussions in depriving Sicilia of an heir to the throne and damaging its relations with Bohemia. Shakespeare forcefully portrays the personal costs of jealousy, not just on Leontes' innocent wife and children but on Leontes himself, as he descends into barely coherent rage and paranoia. The destructive power of his jealousy is thrown into relief by the sexual rivalry of Mopsa and Dorcas, which revisits the theme in comic mode and in a minor key.

Pause for Thought

Consider in what ways the marriage of Leontes and Hermione is contrasted with others that we hear of. Does that of Paulina and Antigonus really fit the stereotype of shrewish wife and hen-pecked husband, or does it seem based on mutual respect? (She still mourns his loss 16 years after his death.) And in what terms does the Shepherd reminisce about his wife?

Idealism of love

In total contrast, we are shown the idealism of love, as seen in the relationship of Florizel and Perdita. Their love overrides all other considerations, whether of family, social class differences, or political concerns. Both express their love in language of striking poetic beauty, and it is their constancy that is perhaps most impressive. When disaster strikes, Florizel claims his love is merely 'delayed,/But nothing altered' (IV.4.442–43), while Perdita responds to Camillo's suggestion that love is altered by 'affliction' with the statement: 'affliction may subdue the cheek,/But not take in the mind' (IV.4.555–56). Later, Florizel asserts that their ill fortune has 'power no jot/…to change our loves' (V.1.216–17).

Repentance

Love is one of the agents of the play's positive outcome; another is Leontes' repentance. At the end of Act III scene 2 he promises that daily penance at the tomb of his wife and son will be his 'recreation' (III.2.235–39), and re-creation indeed turns out to be what his 16 years of 'saint-like sorrow' (V.1.2) achieve. Cleomenes thinks he has done enough, that he has redeemed all his faults and offered more penitence than his sins merited (V.1.1–6), a sentiment later echoed by Camillo (V.3.49–53), but the sight of Hermione's statue has 'conjured to remembrance' his 'evils' (V.3.40), confirming his continued penitence. Cleomenes told him that he needed to 'forgive' himself (V.1.6), but it is Hermione's forgiveness that his self-abasement before her statue — 'I am ashamed' (V.3.37) — earns him. Her forgiveness is made explicit not in words but in her embracing him (V.3.111), and her restoration to life is the concluding element in the play's denouement, which is one of reconciliation between those who were split apart by Leontes' jealousy.

> Love is one of the agents of the play's positive outcome; another is Leontes' repentance

Childhood

Another positive force within the play is childhood. On the one hand Shakespeare offers us examples of very realistically presented children. Mamillius is bright, lively and engaging, but also troublesome to his mother through his very energy. He is more than an idealised conception of youth. Similarly, Florizel and Perdita are invested with sufficient individuality to prevent them being merely representative, abstract figures. The perils and pains of childbirth are also acknowledged. In Jacobean times there was no guarantee that either mother or child would survive the process. Emilia speaks of Hermione's baby as being 'lusty and like to live'. One of the miseries of Hermione's position is that she is rushed to court before she has properly recovered ('strength of limit').

The play sets up an opposition between court and country

Leontes and Polixenes also acknowledge the appeal of childhood. Their mutual recollections at the beginning of the play stress the innocence of their younger days together: 'We were as twinned lambs that did frisk i' th' sun' (I.2.67). It is that lost innocence that Florizel and Perdita recapture in Bohemia. Reconciliation and rebirth are achieved in significant part through the influence of the young.

Social and political themes

Court and country

The play sets up an opposition between court and country, something Shakespeare had explored previously, notably in *As You Like It*. On the face of it, the Sicilian court seems to be presented as a claustrophobic hotbed of festering passions and tyrannous rule, while rural Bohemia is portrayed as a life-affirming, celebratory environment in which generosity and love can flourish. Examined more closely, however, the play's two worlds are more complex: the world of the court contains notable examples of courage and virtue, and that of the country is marred by jealousy, dishonesty and ignorance. As a princess raised to be a shepherdess, Perdita is a symbolic embodiment of the best of both worlds, though had she not been a princess the marital union of court and country would have been socially unthinkable.

Social class

This raises the issue of social class, which is made explicit principally in Polixenes' attitude to his son's relationship with a shepherdess. Though he and Camillo both recognise Perdita's innate qualities — she is 'of most rare note' (IV.2.33–34), and 'Nothing she does or seems/But smacks of something greater than herself' (IV.4.157–58) — her low social status is enough for her to be classified contemptuously as 'a sheep-hook' (IV.4.399) who is 'Worthy enough a herdsman' (IV.4.414). Leontes' reaction to Perdita is interesting: he laments that Florizel's 'choice is not so rich in worth as beauty' (V.1.213), as if 'worth' were a quality reserved for those of elevated social status, yet he still goes on to express his own sexual attraction towards her (V.1.222–23).

Within these assumptions about class, the rise of the Shepherd's family is an interesting illustration of the possibility of upward social mobility in Elizabethan and Jacobean England, first through their acquisition of wealth and finally through the courtly patronage that raises them to the gentry. Autolycus, conversely, illustrates the dangers of a descent in the social scale, in his decline from a member of the prince's retinue to a 'masterless man', obliged to live by begging and criminal behaviour.

Justice

The idea of justice is also widely explored within the play. As in *King Lear*, *The Winter's Tale* dramatically engages with the distinction between justice and law. The terrible, and to many audiences unjust, conclusion of *King Lear* is, in this later play, replaced by a more merciful final judgement on both the guilty and innocent. Leontes promises Hermione a 'just and open trial', but his words and actions both before and after this undertaking cast doubt upon the sincerity of his pledge. Indeed, Hermione, confronted in court by his furious rage, fears she will suffer 'rigour and not law'. Leontes' defiance of a higher justice and the immediate consequences of that defiance bring him shuddering to his senses: 'Apollo's angry, and the heavens themselves/Do strike at my injustice' (III.2.143–44). His acceptance of his guilt and his willingness to undergo a lengthy process of reparation and repentance allow a conclusion where time can bring about reconciliation and redemption.

Religious and philosophical themes

Art and nature

The opposition between court and country finds more abstract expression in the debate between the relative merits of art and nature, a subject of much interest in Shakespeare's time which may seem academic to us today. However, as articulated in Perdita's and Polixenes' discussion on the ethical acceptability of grafting, the debate relates directly to modern anxieties about such issues as genetic modification, cloning and stem cell research, with their emotive language of 'Frankenstein foods' and 'designer babies'. Nature seems to be one of the play's presiding deities. It is invoked by Paulina as 'good goddess Nature' (II.3.103) and by Perdita as 'great creating nature' (IV.4.88), but as Polixenes points out, there is no art that 'adds to nature' that is not in itself 'an art/That nature makes'; thus 'The art itself is nature' (IV.4.88–97). Ultimately, the play seems to endorse Polixenes' viewpoint, with its statue scene that represents a complex interaction of art, even invoking the name of the supposed sculptor, Julio Romano (V.2.77), and nature. The scene is also, of course, a piece of theatre — an art that, according to Hamlet, holds 'the mirror up to nature' (*Hamlet*, III.2.22).

*Pause for **Thought***

Consider this view of the play: 'The play is about the process of social change in seventeenth-century England: the division between court and country, the mastery of nature by the arts of man, the toughness of traditional rural life in the face of political change, the hope for a regenerated England through a reunion of court with cottage, the acceptance of the processes of history' (Charles Barber, in A. Kettle (ed.) *Shakespeare in a Changing World*, 1964).

Religion

Few would interpret *The Winter's Tale* as an explicitly Christian play, least of all in any narrow doctrinal sense. It owes as much to Greek mythology and pagan fertility rituals as it does to any specific relationship with the official orthodoxy of Jacobean Protestantism, though there are occasional Christian references placed carefully in its pre-Christian world, such as allusions to original sin and Judas's betrayal of Jesus. In the broadest sense, though, religion plays a key role in the overall scheme of the play. The play's structure is partly based on the Christian patterning of sin, penance and redemption, and one of its most frequently used words is 'grace', suggesting the divine blessings granted to those who lead holy lives. The word is often spoken by, or associated with, Hermione, whose 'resurrection' has overtones of Christian belief, and its derivatives, 'gracious' and 'disgrace', are also used. There is a sense of sacred ritual in Cleomenes' and Dion's account of the oracle and in the statue scene, while Paulina's injunction to the assembled company, 'It is required/You do awake your faith' (V.3.94–95), sets the seal on the play's religious suggestiveness.

Time

Time is…a central preoccupation of the play

This is also a central preoccupation of the play, not just in its personification as chorus, but in its persistent evocation through various strands of the imagery. Time, with the possibility it brings for growth and regeneration, is a significant theme in all the 'last plays'. Units of time mentioned in *The Winter's Tale* vary from the 'hours [and] minutes' that, according to Leontes, illicit lovers wish to pass more swiftly (I.2.289–90) to the 'Nine changes of the wat'ry star' (I.2.1) of Polixenes' visit and Hermione's pregnancy; from the 16-year 'wide gap of time' (V.3.154) covered by the play's narrative, to the Shepherd's 'fourscore three' years of age (IV.4.432). We are also taken back in time 'twenty-three years' (I.2.155) to the childhood friendship of Leontes and Polixenes, and forward to the concept of 'perpetuity' (I.2.5). Time is implicit too in the play's seasonal imagery with its reference to the natural cycles of birth, growth, death and renewal, highlighted by the allusion to the myth of Proserpina (IV.4.116). Ultimately, it is the cyclical nature of human life that the play invokes, both morally and physically. Time deals out 'both joy and terror/Of good and bad [and] makes and unfolds error' (IV.1.1–2); it also determines the repetitive process by which 'things dying' are succeeded by 'things new born' (III.3.100–01). No wonder Leontes asks Paulina to 'Hastily lead away' at the end of the play (V.3.155) in his anxiety to enjoy what has been restored to him before time revokes it.

Top ten *quotation*>

Paulina, hinting that he has privately expressed an interest in marrying her: 'For him, I partly know his mind' (V.3.142).

It is difficult to question Leontes' final assessment of Camillo's 'worth and honesty' which can be 'justified/By…a pair of kings' (V.3.144–46), but a good actor in the role will also have shown during the play a character driven partly by self-preservation and self-interest.

Paulina

Entirely Shakespeare's invention, Paulina is a pivotal figure in the scheme of the play. Though partly conceived as the sharp-tongued shrewish wife, or scold, she transcends the stereotypical features of such roles to become a powerful advocate for truth and justice. Her authority is evident on her very first appearance, as she orders her attendants to summon the Gaoler, whom she assumes will jump to attention on hearing her name: 'Let him have knowledge who I am' (II.2.2). She is forthright, outspoken and determined, not afraid to speak openly of the king's 'dangerous, unsafe lunes' (II.2.30) and confident of her own power over him: 'He must be told on't, and he shall. The office/Becomes a woman best; I'll take't upon me' (II.2.31–32).

Shakespeare is careful to make it clear how Paulina is regarded in the court: the Gaoler knows her for 'a worthy lady,/And one who much I honour' (II.2.5–6), while Emilia also calls her 'worthy', praises her 'honour' and 'goodness', and asserts that 'There is no lady living/So meet for this great errand' (II.2.42–46).

Paulina's behaviour in the remainder of Acts I–III builds on the expectations aroused in this introductory scene, showing her moral and physical courage in action as she dominates the court in her two powerful confrontations with Leontes. In Act II scene 3 she bursts into his presence despite the lords' protestations, professing to be the 'physician' (II.3.54) who will 'bring him sleep' (II.3.33), courageously resisting all attempts to remove her from the chamber by force (II.3.61–64, 124–26), and contemptuously rebuffing his threats to have her burnt: 'I care not:/It is an heretic that makes the fire,/Not she which burns in't' (II.3.113–14). She also brings comedy into the play, at Leontes' expense, beginning with his rueful rebuke to Antigonus, 'I charged thee that she should not come about me./I knew she would' (II.3.43–44).

Paulina performs a more serious function, however, in her announcement of the queen's death, which she delays with rhetorical skill for the space of 27 lines. During this she takes the opportunity

Pause for **Thought**

How far do you agree with the view of the nineteenth-century writer Hartley Coleridge that 'Camillo is an old rogue whom I can hardly forgive for his double treachery'? (1851)

to give Leontes a powerful resumé of his stupidity and wickedness, accompanied by sarcasm and insult. In retrospect, there is an irony in her exhortation of Leontes not to 'repent these things' (III.2.205), since the gods will never grant him forgiveness even if he spends 10,000 years in painful penance. In the event, it only takes 16 years for him to be redeemed, at least in human terms.

Sixteen years later it appears as if Paulina's role in Leontes' court has become that of guardian of Hermione's memory. Time may have mellowed her, but she is still adept at using her linguistic skill to prick Leontes' conscience, painfully referring to Hermione as 'she you killed' (V.1.15), and continuing to draw rebukes from the courtiers for her lack of tact and diplomacy (V.1.20–23). There is a sense of urgency to her constant reminders of Hermione's qualities, since there is political pressure on the king to remarry, and her evocation of the late queen's vengeful ghost, 'shriek[ing]' in passionate bitterness at any new wife (V.1.56–67), has the same grotesque quality as Antigonus's vision of Hermione in Act III scene 3. Only now does Shakespeare begin to hint, through Paulina, that Hermione is not dead. Making Leontes swear 'never to marry but by [her] free leave' (V.1.70), she imagines a new queen 'not…so young/As was your former' who will only exist 'when your first queen's again in breath' (V.1.78–83).

Paulina is a consummate master of ceremonies in the final scene

Paulina is a consummate master of ceremonies in the final scene, yet paradoxically she seems humbler and more restrained than anywhere else in the play, thanking Leontes and Polixenes for visiting her 'poor house' (V.3.6) and offering a moving apology for all her former behaviour: 'What…/I did not well, I meant well' (V.3.2–3). She manages the gradual build-up of suspense with subtlety and skill, tempting her audience to demand more even while threatening to end the performance, three times attempting to close the curtain that has revealed the statue (V.3.59, 68 and 83). As she moves to the climax of her show, she is eager to deny the involvement of 'wicked powers' and disclaims that she is engaged in 'unlawful business' (V.3.91 and 96) — a reminder, perhaps, that Leontes once referred to her as a 'mankind witch' (II.3.67). When Hermione finally moves, it is under direct instruction from Paulina, who is required to speak stage directions to all the characters at this point, such is their wonder: she tells Leontes to present his hand to his wife (V.3.107), Perdita to kneel to her mother (V.3.119–20) and Hermione to turn to her daughter (V.3.120). Paulina ends her spoken role with wry self-pity, contrasting herself with the 'precious winners all' (V.3.131) and lamenting her own old age and widowhood (V.3.132–35). When she is unexpectedly offered the hand of Camillo, Shakespeare gives her no response, leaving an actor to determine how she feels;

but her key role in the play is recognised by Leontes who, against the normal conventions of precedence in a dramatic exit, invites her to 'Hastily lead away' the assembled company (V.3.155).

Autolycus

Autolycus erupts into the play with invigorating energy; after the solemnity of the preceding events, the last thing we expect is a singing con-man, particularly when we have just been led to anticipate an introduction to Florizel and Perdita. His cheerful amorality acts as a corrective to events in Sicilia; compared with the psychotic cruelty of Leontes, his criminality is trivial and even admirable, particularly as no one genuinely suffers as a result of his activities. Shakespeare offers us enough details about his life and background to give him an air of reality — his former service of Florizel (IV.3.13–14), his inheriting of his trade from his father (IV.3.23–25), his evocation of the all-too-real dangers of his way of life (IV.3.27–28) and his local reputation (IV.3.87–88); essentially, though, we take him at face value.

Autolycus has only two big opportunities to work the audience: in his fleecing of the Clown and his incarnation as the ballad-monger. After this, his singing is silenced and he himself becomes largely an instrument of the plot. Dramatically, his role goes into decline, and he is only restored to something of his old self in his mockery of the Shepherd and Clown at the end of Act IV scene 4. However, since their world has now crumbled about their ears, Autolycus's trickery no longer has quite the same sense of fun. By Act V he is reduced to being the silent recipient of the Gentlemen's narrative revelations, before being bested by his erstwhile victims. It is a surprising dramatic falling-off, marked by his ignominious verbal submission in promising to 'amend [his] life' (V.2.124) and 'prove' a 'tall fellow of [his] hands' (V.2.136–38). For an actor, this must be frustrating; for the play, it is vital: a lively musical climax for Autolycus would detract from the solemn impact of the concluding scene.

Perdita

Like Miranda in *The Tempest*, Perdita can appear somewhat insipid. Unlike the heroines of Shakespeare's other last plays, Marina in *Pericles* and Imogen in *Cymbeline*, she is not faced with physical and moral hazards that she has to confront for herself, since she always has Florizel beside her. Her modesty (IV.4.9), her unease at the 'borrowed flaunts'

Taking it Further ▶
....
Read Louis MacNeice's poem 'Autolycus' (printed on pp. 108–10 of the Cambridge School Shakespeare edition of the play) and consider how MacNeice uses the character to reflect on Shakespeare himself and his final plays.
....

*Pause for **Thought***
What do you think is Autolycus's most important dramatic function?

(IV.4.23) of her role as festive hostess, her anxiety about the outcome of her relationship with the prince (IV.4.35–40), her shyness (IV.4.67), her condemnation of botanical interbreeding (IV.4.86–88), her romantic flower poetry (IV.4.116–29) and her prim concern about the possible scurrility of the pedlar's songs (IV.4.207) all diminish her appeal to a modern audience. In Shakespeare's time, however, they would probably have been regarded as glowing testimonials to her feminine virtues.

There is little material in her role to make her into a more feisty heroine, but plenty to reduce her status as a model of virtue. She is, after all, engaged in a serious deception with unpredictable domestic and political consequences, and her courage when the inevitable crisis occurs (IV.4.421–25) is marked by a singular failure to address any explanation to her foster-father; no wonder he calls her 'cursèd wretch' (IV.4.437) before he leaves in despair. To Florizel she can only say the equivalent of 'I told you so' (IV.4.453), and her brave words about moral courage (IV.4.555–56) are spoken in a virtual vacuum, being two of fewer than ten lines that she speaks in the space of the 218 during which Florizel and Camillo organise a course of action. In Act V she speaks only three times: once, at last, to express sympathy for the Shepherd — while also bewailing her own misfortune (V.1.201–03); once to kneel and beg the blessing of Hermione's statue (V.3.42–46); and once to echo Leontes' willingness to gaze at it for 20 years (V.3.84–85). The climax of her role, her response to her mother's reanimation, is silent but steeped in emotion.

What all this reveals, in part, is the different expectations that we may have of a dramatic character from those prevalent in Shakespeare's time. Perdita is essentially character as symbol, and her function in the play does not require us to respond to her as a complex or even sympathetic human being: it is what she represents, rather than her personality, that is important. She is the lost child found, the agent of reconciliation, the restorer of marital and political harmony.

Florizel

Florizel is a flawed hero (see the comments in the *Scene summaries and commentaries* section on Act IV scene 4 on pp. 23–29), but again we must be careful of judging his role by modern standards of characterisation. Romantic, passionate, courageous and resourceful, his optimistic imagery works alongside that of Autolycus, whose opening song declared that 'the red blood reigns in the winter's pale' (IV.3.4), to evoke a mood of joyful celebration. 'Apprehend/Nothing but jollity,' declares Florizel (IV.4.24–25), and urges Perdita: 'let's be red with mirth' (IV.4.54).

Pause for Thought ⏸

A number of modern productions have doubled the roles of Perdita and Hermione — most notably when Judi Dench played both parts in Trevor Nunn's 1969 RSC production. What would such a decision add to the play? What difficulties would it present in the final scene, and how might these be overcome?

Like Perdita, however, he demonstrates no sympathy for the Shepherd's distress; indeed, he immediately follows the old man's exit with the guiltily defensive 'Why look you so upon me?' (IV.4.441), before affirming his determination not to cave in to his father's anger. Already well practised in deception, he carries off his arrival in Leontes' court in the role of Bohemian ambassador with persuasive diplomatic skill. These features of his character all serve to humanise him, so that we do not see him as an idealised fairy-tale figure, but it is important for the overall scheme of the play that he comes across essentially as a worthy match for Perdita, whose faults can be put down to his youth and to the admirable constancy of his love, which is not bound by the artificial dictates of social class barriers.

The story of Perdita and Florizel appealed to nineteenth-century sentiment, as shown in this illustration from Charles and Mary Lamb's *Tales from Shakespeare* (1807)

At all his key moments Florizel gains our approval. His optimism is infectious; his promise of chastity (IV.4.33–35) demonstrates his respect for Perdita; his praise of her qualities is expressed in some of the play's loveliest poetry (IV.4.135–46); his participation in the feasting and dancing shows his social skills to be free of all condescension; and his various expressions of love and constancy are forceful and impressive (e.g. IV.4.466–71, V.1.214–17). Some of the verse Shakespeare gives him is so powerful in its imagery that it would not be out of place on the lips of one of his tragic heroes, notably when he asserts that if he violates his faith, 'then/Let nature crush the sides o'th'earth together/ And mar the seeds within!' (IV.4.456–58). He shows enormous warmth in his dealings with Camillo, and his willingness to take the advice of his father's trusted counsellor demonstrates humility and gratitude. He can even make a joke of their situation: 'Should I now meet my father,/He would not call me son' (IV.4.626–27). His dignity when he believes Camillo has betrayed him and he is forced to ask for Leontes' help and support is notable (V.1.217–21), and his courage and faithful love never waver. Shakespeare gives him no words during the final scene of the play, but his presence needs to be strongly felt in his physical relationship with Perdita, maintaining the love and support he has shown throughout as she deals with the emotional impact of her mother's restoration.

Lebrecht Music and Arts Photo Library/Alamy

Task 8

Only some of the main characters have been considered here. Make a case for the importance to the play of one other character.

Form, structure and language

This section is designed to offer you information about the three strands of AO2. This Assessment Objective requires you to demonstrate detailed critical understanding in analysing the ways in which form, structure and language shape meanings in literary texts. To a certain extent these three terms should, as indicated elsewhere, be seen as fluid and interactive. Remember, however, that in the analysis of a play such as *The Winter's Tale* aspects of form and structure are at least as important as language. You should certainly not focus your study merely on lexical features of the text. Many features of form, structure and language in *The Winter's Tale* are further explored elsewhere in scene summaries and sample essays.

Form

The Winter's Tale has at different times been variously categorised as a tragicomedy, a romance, a late play and a problem play. Generic categories, however, are not fixed. Genres can be variously defined, overlap, and are constantly in a state of flux. To label *The Winter's Tale* simply as a romance, for instance, may be to undervalue the realistic way the play depicts character and events. It is, anyway, often hazardous to try to force Shakespeare's plays into a particular compartment.

Nevertheless, it is easy to identify many of the characteristic features of tragedy in the first half of *The Winter's Tale*. It has often been pointed out that if the play had concluded with Act III scene 2, it would have fulfilled many of the expectations of a tragedy, with Leontes condemned to a sort of death-in-life. Leontes plays the part of a traditional tragic protagonist in that his own weakness and error bring down destruction on himself and those around him. He finds himself increasingly isolated and he lacks self-knowledge and understanding of the world in which he lives. Human society seems unable to protect itself against the onrush of evil; madness supplants sanity, and Sicilia finds itself contemplating terrible waste and loss. However, the whole direction of the play alters at its midway point, and takes on a very different form.

Leontes plays the part of a traditional tragic protagonist in that his own weakness and error bring down destruction

Shakespeare's last plays

When Shakespeare began work around 1608 on what we now think of as his last plays, he was striking out in a new direction. Since the turn of the century, he had focused on a series of powerful but diverse tragedies; he had interspersed these with two dark, ironic comedies, *Measure for Measure* and *All's Well that Ends Well*, exploring complex moral issues with only partial or ambiguous resolutions, and with the bitterly satirical drama of love and war, *Troilus and Cressida*. In the plays that followed, though, the potential for tragedy is diverted into a series of positive outcomes, as Shakespeare embraces the increasingly popular genre of tragicomedy. These plays have a great deal in common with each other, including some striking verbal echoes.

Presumably, when Shakespeare began writing *Pericles* in about 1607–08, he did not consciously consider that he was embarking upon his final sequence of plays. In retrospect, however, critics have seen it as the first of a group of related works with which he closed his career as a dramatist. The plays in this group consist essentially of the four 'romances', *Pericles, Cymbeline, The Winter's Tale* and *The Tempest*. There can be no doubt of the many similarities between these plays, some of which are outlined below. However, these parallels have perhaps been given too much weight in the past, obscuring the fact that the differences between the plays are just as striking as their similarities, and that there are also frequent parallels with plays written much earlier in Shakespeare's career.

Similarities between the last plays

The principal parallels between these plays lie in their plots, characters, themes and imagery. Children are separated from their royal parents, often in ignorance of their own true identities, but finally reunited. Evil acts committed in corrupt courtly societies are mitigated by a transfer of the characters to idealised rural landscapes or remote islands. The qualities of particular flowers are celebrated as they are 'strewn' on the dead and the living. Characters repent their sins and are rewarded by reconciliation with those they wronged, including at least three wives and one husband who had been thought dead. Characters are battered by storm and tempest, but the elements that threatened eventually prove merciful. Dreams, visions and prophecies relate the stories to a legendary world ruled by the gods: Diana and Jupiter make dramatic personal appearances, Apollo's voice is heard through his oracle, and Iris, Ceres and Juno are conjured up in a magical wedding celebration. Loyal old counsellors stand firm against tyranny and offer moral guidance and

Taking it Further ▶

Read or watch a performance of *The Tempest*. What significant points of contrast and comparison can you find with *The Winter's Tale*?

Context

The genre of tragicomedy was popular in the early years of the seventeenth century. The King's Men, in particular, led the fashion in this respect, not only with Shakespeare's plays but with other popular works such as Beaumont and Fletcher's *Philaster* (1609) and *A King and No King* (1611); other companies soon joined the bandwagon.

*Pause for **Thought*** ⏸

How applicable to *The Winter's Tale* is the idea that tragedy can be distinguished from tragicomedy through the treatment of death as described here?

practical advice. The mistakes of the old are rectified by the love and energy of their children. Tragedy is shown to be only a partial response to a life in which the natural cycle brings rebirth, regeneration or, as Leontes calls it, 'recreation' (III.2.237). Winter must always be succeeded by spring. The happy endings, though, remain provisional: not all those who die along the way can be reborn, and not all the evil characters can be brought to embrace repentance and forgiveness.

Tragicomedy

Tragicomedy has at times been regarded as an inferior genre, lacking both the joyous exuberance of comedy and the philosophical seriousness of tragedy. It has been defined in many ways, but it is usually thought of as combining elements of tragedy and comedy either through the provision of a harmonious ending to a story that had seemed to be heading towards tragedy, or through mixing light and serious elements throughout the play.

Treatment of death

One way in which tragicomedy has been distinguished from tragedy is through its treatment of death. Whereas tragedy conventionally ends with the death of the central protagonist, tragicomedy often places a dramatic emphasis on the danger of death, but a death from which the central characters escape.

Romance and pastoral modes

Associated with tragicomedy were the literary modes of romance, dealing with unrealistic episodes often involving lovers; and pastoral, set in an idealised country landscape inhabited by shepherds and their flocks. Both modes can be seen at work in *The Winter's Tale*, though Shakespeare had used them much earlier in *As You Like It* (1600), a play that has a great deal in common with these later works. The plot of *The Winter's Tale* also contains strong parallels with another earlier comedy, *Much Ado about Nothing* (1598–99).

Resolution

Shakespeare's use of Time as the chorus to *The Winter's Tale* points up another issue about genre. It is implicit in Time's speech that healing and regeneration are not the end — merely the arbitrary conclusion imposed for the purposes of the genres known as 'comedy' or 'tragicomedy'. Time makes it clear that he controls 'both joy and terror/Of good and bad', and that he 'makes' as well as 'unfolds' error (IV.1.1–2). Shakespeare ends most of his comedies with a sense that the comedic closure is only provisional, undercutting the final harmony with unsettling elements. What kind of a marriage is in store for Benedick and Beatrice in *Much Ado about Nothing* or Helena and Bertram in *All's Well that Ends Well?* 'All yet seems well' says the King at the end of that play; perhaps the same linguistic qualification — 'seems' rather than 'is' — needs to be applied to all of Shakespeare's so-called 'happy endings', including *The Winter's Tale*. The section on Act V scene 3 in the *Scene summaries and commentaries* (on pp. 33–35 of this guide) examines some of the ambiguous undercurrents that potentially darken the resolution of this play.

Taking it
Further

Many critics have explored the masque-like qualities of Act IV scene 4. Court masques became very popular in the reign of James I. Find out what you can about these entertainments and discuss what elements of the masque appear in this scene.

Structure

There are several different ways of considering the structure of *The Winter's Tale*.

Three movements

One view can see the play as almost symphonic in its creation of three movements, each with its own particular mood, but with echoes of the others interwoven throughout. The first movement, consisting of Acts I–III, is a bold and passionate statement of Leontes' irrational jealousy. In its final scene, the baby's rescue by shepherds sows the seeds for the pastoral second movement in Act IV. The low-key beginning of Act IV is soon succeeded by the celebratory mood of the sheep-shearing festival, with Autolycus and Perdita as its contrasting presiding spirits. Echoes of the first movement emerge in Polixenes' violent anger, but there are enough hints of a positive resolution to prevent this from being the dominant mood. Act V, the play's third and final movement, is subdued, steeped in an air of spiritual sadness that develops into the transcendental joys of forgiveness and reconciliation. As in a symphony, leitmotifs from all the previous movements recur here.

Two parts

These three movements are unequal in length, and in modern productions the play is usually performed in two parts, with an interval after Act III. We do not know whether intervals were taken at outdoor theatres such as the Globe, though many plays of the period do build up to a point about three-fifths of the way through that seems designed for such a break. In *The Winter's Tale* this coincides with the play's 'wide gap of time', and Time's chorus is a striking and apt way to pick up the story after an intermission.

Five acts

Shakespeare carefully subdivides the opening movement of *The Winter's Tale* to cater for the five-act structure. With the first scene as a kind of prologue, Act I provides the play's exposition, setting up Leontes' jealousy and preparing the ground for his confrontation with Hermione. Act II sees Leontes in conflict with all around him, and it reaches a climax with the removal of the baby to its fate. Act III focuses on Hermione's trial and its dramatic conclusion, but is framed by two quite different scenes — first, the calm description of the oracle and finally, the storm-tossed arrival of the baby on the Bohemian coast, the destruction of the agents of its exposure and its rescue by the Shepherd and Clown.

Acts IV and V are carefully structured and paced. Act IV, for example, begins with an unexpected chorus that makes way for the flatly written scene between Polixenes and Camillo, which is engineered deliberately to enhance the impact of Autolycus's freewheeling incursion into the action. Act V scene 1 builds carefully towards the play's anticipated denouement, only to toy with the audience in the anticlimactic discussion between the three Gentlemen in order to heighten the surprise ending. Perhaps the only moment in the play when Shakespeare's pacing falters is at the end of Act IV scene 4, when Florizel and Perdita's escape plans take a disproportionate amount of time to establish, which dissipates the dramatic tension that has been built up.

The play, then, has a number of alternative structures layered one on top of another: two parts, three movements, five acts, and each act carefully structured with its own dramatic shape geared to the rhythms of the whole play.

Advantages and disadvantages of the time gap

Some considerations of the structure of the play have been more negative. The 16-year gap has not always met with critical approval; it has been seen as awkwardly artificial, and dividing the play into two halves which drift away from each other. There are, however, counter-arguments that Shakespeare establishes many connections between the two halves of the play that help to create a sense of dramatic unity, such as the part played by Camillo, a threat posed by a jealous king, and the sea journey that Perdita is forced to endure. Another argument, when

Context

Structuring of plays at the indoor Blackfriars theatre demanded a distinctive dramatic framework, with regular breaks to trim the candles that lit the theatre. The five-act structure familiar from printed play texts probably developed to serve this need; indeed, there is evidence that some of the King's Men's existing plays were revised to this end when they began to perform at the Blackfriars, for example Shakespeare's *Measure for Measure*, which was probably restructured by Thomas Middleton.

comparing the play to *The Tempest*, is that the device of Time and the 16-year gap allow the audience to witness the effects of the passage of time, rather than the somewhat awkward early scenes in *The Tempest* when a long narrative is required to explain the events that led to Miranda's presence on the island.

A representation of the seasons

Another way of looking at the structure of the play is as a representation of the pattern of the seasons. The play begins in winter, as identified by Mamillius at the beginning of Act II, 'A sad tale's best for winter', and metaphorically represented in the harshness and sterility that overtakes the Sicilian court. A Lenten period of fast and repentance follows before the fourth act brings both spring-like imagery of swallows and daffodils and the rich plenty of summer and autumn harvest. The arrival of Florizel and Perdita to what is still a wintry Sicilia is like the coming of 'the spring to th' earth' (V.1.151), and the ending of the play anticipates the renewal of the natural cycle.

Language

Verse and prose

Verse is language that is organised rhythmically according to particular patterns of metre and the arrangement of lines. In plays of Shakespeare's time and earlier, verse was the conventional medium of dramatic discourse. Plays were not regarded as naturalistic slices of life, and the heightened language of verse was felt to be appropriate to their non-realistic status as performance texts. However, dramatists increasingly varied the range of their dramatic language to include speeches and scenes in prose, the language of everyday speech and writing. Verse tended to be given to noble and royal characters, expressing romantic or elevated feelings, while prose was generally used by characters of lower social status, for comic or domestic scenes, for letters read out loud, or to indicate mental disturbance. In *The Winter's Tale* approximately one-third of the play is in prose, and two-thirds in verse.

Verse

By the start of Shakespeare's career, one particular verse metre had come to dominate the language of plays. This was based on a line

Task 9

Another way of exploring the structure of the text is to look at the pattern of appearances of the main characters. Construct a grid or chart in which you mark the scenes in which the different characters appear. Are there any significant patterns to their appearances or equally significant 'groupings' of characters?

of ten syllables, arranged so that the beats, or stresses, fell on every second syllable. Thus, each line consisted of five units (or metrical feet), each consisting of an unstressed syllable followed by a stressed one, as follows:

~ /　~ /　~ /　~ /　~ /

Each of these units is called an iambic foot, and since there are five of them in each line, the metre is called iambic pentameter. Here are two typical examples from the play:

~　/　~　/　~　/　~　/　~　/
To tell | he longs | to see | his son | were strong.　　(I.2.34)

~ /　~　/　~　/　~　/　~　/
I am | appoint | ed him | to mur | der you.　　(I.2.412)

In the earlier drama of the time, including Shakespeare's first plays, the rhythms of the iambic pentameter tended to be kept very regular, at the risk of becoming monotonous. As Shakespeare's career developed, he became more flexible in his use of this basic metre.

As Shakespeare's career developed, he became more flexible in his use of…metre

Again, in early plays, each verse line tended to be a unit of meaning. Later in his career, Shakespeare much more frequently ran the sense of one line into the next, a technique called enjambement; he also created more heavy breaks in the middle of a line, known as caesuras. Both of these have the effect of obscuring rather than emphasising the underlying rhythm of the lines. Look, for example, at this speech of Leontes, where the frequent use of enjambement, caesura and metrical irregularity all help to destroy the rhythms of the verse and suggest Leontes' disturbed state of mind:

> **Nor night nor day no rest. It is but weakness**
> **To bear the matter thus, mere weakness. If**
> **The cause were not in being — part o'th'cause,**
> **She, th'adultress; for the harlot king**
> **Is quite beyond mine arm, out of the blank**
> **And level of my brain, plot-proof; but she**
> **I can hook to me — say that she were gone,**
> **Given to the fire, a moiety of my rest**
> **Might come to me again. Who's there?**　　(II.3.1–9)

In *The Winter's Tale*, the basic verse contains absolutely no rhyme at all. Iambic pentameter without any rhymes is called blank verse, and this is the standard verse form of the play. The only use of rhyme in the play is for two particular purposes:

- the songs, which are in a variety of verse forms; and
- the speech of Time, which is in iambic pentameter and rhyming couplets

Prose

Most of Shakespeare's plays contain sections in prose as well as verse, and *The Winter's Tale* is no exception.

It is a mistake to think that prose is somehow more naturalistic or realistic than verse. Prose can encompass the language of novels, textbooks, newspapers, magazines, letters, diaries and legal documents, and it can be as structured and artificial as verse. It is the everyday language, in speech and writing, of people of varying degrees of education and literacy, and is consequently infinitely varied in its rhythms, grammatical structures and vocabulary.

In *The Winter's Tale*, the following sections are in prose:

- the opening scene — the conversation between Camillo and Archidamus (I.1)
- the indictment against Hermione (III.2.12–19)
- the dialogue between the Shepherd and the Clown (III.3.58–119)
- the scene between Polixenes and Camillo (IV.2)
- the scene between Autolycus and the Clown (IV.3)
- the entertainments within the sheep-shearing scene (IV.4.181–321) — except for the songs
- most of the conclusion of the scene, from the re-entry of Autolycus (IV.4.574–780), though the courtly characters, other than Camillo, stick to verse
- the scene between Autolycus and the Gentlemen, Shepherd and Clown (V.2)

For all the above sections of the play, you need to consider a range of issues relating to the use of prose, such as:

- What kind of characters are speaking, and in what context?
- Do these characters use prose throughout the play? If not, why do they use it here?
- What precedes or follows each prose section? Does the prose have the effect of lowering the dramatic temperature after a verse scene? Does it heighten the impact of a verse scene that follows? Or does it simply provide a contrast of tone?

- What kind of prose is it? Is it elaborate, courtly and artificial, or rustic, colloquial and comic? Does it employ long, complex, balanced sentences or short, straightforward ones? What linguistic devices does it employ, and what effects do these create?

Imagery

An image is the mental picture conjured up by a particular word or phrase. When writers use related patterns or clusters of images, they are using imagery as a literary technique. Such imagery may serve a number of purposes: it may be a feature of characterisation, infusing characters with particular associations; it may contribute to the creation of mood and atmosphere; or it may support the thematic significance of the text.

It can be misleading to generalise about Shakespeare's imagery, but it is useful to recognise the broad contrast in its use between the tragedies and the comedies.

- In the tragedies, the imagery tends to create unpleasant emotive associations. Violence, blood, disease, darkness, evil and the supernatural, lust and appetite walk hand in hand with images of wild animals, winter weather and storm and tempest.
- In the comedies, the overriding images are of love and friendship, spring flowers, birds, calm weather, good health and spirituality, with a particular emphasis on song, dance and music.

When it comes to the last plays, one striking aspect of their imagery is the way it combines the characteristic images of the tragedies and comedies. Images of disease and cure, winter and spring, youth and old age, tempest and music work side by side, suggesting a more inclusive and balanced view of life. All of these opposing image clusters are employed in *The Winter's Tale* as well as the other romances, and seem appropriate for plays that deal in the mode of tragicomedy.

Also significant is the combination of concrete and abstract images whereby Shakespeare is able both to present a vividly realised physical world and to explore the workings of the mind and imagination. Autolycus, for instance, is portrayed both through his own words and those of others as a complex of clothes, movements, words and gaudy items for sale. Leontes' twisted imaginings move from an obsessive focus on the workings of the body to abstract references to disgrace, despair and nothingness.

Task 10

Consider the following key image clusters, giving careful consideration to the effects they create:
- disease and cure
- sleep, sleeplessness and dreams
- the seasons and weather
- birds, animals and flowers
- storm and tempest
- time
- grace and graciousness
- the gods
- nature and natural processes
- youth and old age
- texts, tales and printing

Contexts

This section offers you an insight into the influence of some significant contexts in which *The Winter's Tale* was written, and in which it has been performed and received. Assessment Objective 4 requires demonstration of an understanding of the significance of contexts of production and reception. Such contextual material should, however, be used with caution. Reference to contexts is only valuable when it informs a reading of the text. Contextual material which is clumsily introduced or 'bolted on' to an argument contributes little.

Historical context

Queen Elizabeth and King James

The supreme power of the monarch as head of state was increasingly subject to critical scrutiny as the Tudor age, culminating in the long reign of Elizabeth I, gave way to that of her Stuart successor, James I. Maintaining the political status quo depended on numerous factors, not the least of which was ensuring a clear and strong line of succession. Since Elizabeth was unmarried and childless, anxieties about who would succeed her became acute as she moved into old age and ill health.

The issue of succession in the play

Concern about succession is explored quite openly in *The Winter's Tale*: in many ways the most shocking element in the oracle's pronouncement is that 'the king shall live without an heir, if that which is lost be not found'. The horrible significance of this statement is evidently lost on the lords, who respond 'Now blessèd be the great Apollo!', and even on Hermione, who can only add 'Praised!' (III.2.134). Only when the servant enters to announce Mamillius's death does the actual meaning of the oracle hit home. The play's opening scene had made much of the prince's future potential, ending with the comment 'If the king had no son they would desire to live on crutches till he had one' (I.1.37–38), and in Act I scene 2 it was clear that both Polixenes and Leontes found in their respective sons the chief source of their contentment. When Polixenes later threatens to disinherit Florizel — 'we'll bar thee from

...by Act V the question of succession is central to the political anxieties of the Sicilian lords

succession' (IV.4.408) — it creates a much more profound shock than may be apparent to us, and by Act V the question of succession is central to the political anxieties of the Sicilian lords as they urge Leontes to remarry. The kingdom is 'heirless' (V.1.10) and Leontes 'issueless' (V.1.173), and his stubbornness, supported by Paulina, is a source of intense frustration for his ministers.

During the last years of Elizabeth's reign, some of her courtiers had conducted secret correspondence with her cousin James VI of Scotland, whose mother, Mary, Queen of Scots, Elizabeth had had executed. When the queen died in March 1603, James succeeded peacefully to the English throne; whether Elizabeth formally acknowledged him as heir on her deathbed is disputed. Paulina's statement that 'the crown will find an heir' echoes the attitude taken by Elizabeth, and when she talks of Alexander the Great leaving his crown to 'th'worthiest; so his successor/ Was like to be the best' (V.1.47–49), this might be read by the Jacobean audience as a flattering comment addressed to King James, similar to those Shakespeare had scattered through the text of *Macbeth* just a few years earlier. When Hermione claims in the final scene that she has preserved herself to see 'the issue', she may primarily mean the outcome of events, but the noun is also overlaid with the senses of both 'child' and 'heir', as used so often elsewhere in the play.

Political alliances

In view of the cordial relations between Sicilia and Bohemia, if Leontes' jealousy had not destroyed his family, the prospect of marriage between his daughter and Florizel would have been a likely political alliance. In an interesting historical coincidence, one of Europe's most powerful princes, the Elector Palatine, who married James I's daughter, Elizabeth, in 1613, became King of Bohemia six years later. *The Winter's Tale* was one of 14 plays performed at court in the two months of celebrations before their wedding, and its Bohemian setting would have been particularly resonant when it was played there again in 1618 or 1619.

Social context

Social class

Attitudes to social class in Shakespeare's time seem somewhat contradictory. There was still an assumption that character and social status went hand in hand, so that only aristocrats could demonstrate true nobility. Shakespeare's view seems notably ambivalent: ultimately, Perdita is a fit wife for Florizel only because she is in reality a princess; yet in his portrayal of the Shepherd and Clown Shakespeare makes it clear that human decency, charity and compassion are not qualities confined to the gentry. The play rewards them by their comic elevation to being 'gentlemen born', but perhaps there is a satirical glance here at James I's fondness for issuing knighthoods to his loyal supporters, thus elevating them to a higher place in the social hierarchy.

It is also worth remembering that Shakespeare's father's 20-year ambition to achieve gentlemanly status had finally been achieved in 1596 when he was able to acquire a coat of arms, probably as a result of his son's rapidly growing reputation and increasing financial success. Perhaps, even by 1611, Shakespeare still felt a lingering sense of social stigma attached to his provincial background; after all, in 1592 in an envious attack the playwright Robert Greene had described him as an 'upstart crow', which perhaps related as much to his social status as to his lack of a university education. It was Greene's novel, *Pandosto*, that Shakespeare used as the basis of *The Winter's Tale*.

Religion and mythology

Doctrinal differences

Shakespeare avoids approaching doctrinal religious differences in his plays, and indeed it would have been dangerous to do so, particularly if, as many scholars believe, he and his family were secret adherents of the Catholic faith. Moreover, an act was passed in 1606 'for the preventing and avoiding of the great abuse of the Holy Name of God in stage plays', with a £10 fine incurred for every such offence. Companies were given eight days to expurgate their existing plays, though oblique references were acceptable, as in Polixenes' allusion to Judas's betrayal of Christ (I.2.418–19), which does not name either character. Mocking the Puritans did not count as an offence, of course, and playwrights often did so; the Clown, for example, notes that among the shearers who are to sing at the feast, there is 'one puritan…, and he sings psalms to hornpipes' (IV.3.39–40) — a horrible combination, one is meant to imagine.

Christian theology

Many critics have found an underlying sense of Christian theology in *The Winter's Tale*, despite its ostensibly pagan setting, notably in its powerful structure which follows the central Christian patterning of sin, penance and redemption, with the final stage even marked by a kind of resurrection. Few, however, would go so far as to interpret the whole play as a Christian allegory, in line with S. L. Bethell's belief that it shows that 'Shakespeare's mature interpretation of life is that of the Christian faith' (in *The Winter's Tale: A Study*, 1947).

There is no doubting, though, that there is a sense of genuine spirituality about the play, from the account given by Cleomenes and Dion of Apollo's oracle in Act III scene 1, steeped in the language of religious ritual, to the mood of 'saint-like sorrow' (V.1.2) that invests Leontes' court in Act V, leading to the transcendental wonder of Hermione's restoration to life. Shakespeare distances all this from engagement with controversial ideas of Christian doctrine by placing it in the context of the classical Roman gods and the allegorical figure of Time. The play's religious sensibilities could not be allowed to come too close to home.

Myth and folklore

In fact, Christian theology is no more important in the thematic scheme of the play than myth and folklore. In its exploitation of fertility myths, stressing seasonal renewal, the play owes a particular debt to the story of Proserpina, explicitly referred to by Perdita at IV.4.116. Shakespeare could take for granted in his audience a far greater knowledge of Greek and Roman mythology than most people possess now, and the story was a familiar one, best known from Ovid's *Metamorphoses*, which he frequently used as source material.

The relationship of Proserpina's story to the plot of *The Winter's Tale* works suggestively rather than through parallel storylines. The Sicilian link is convenient, the mother's loss of her daughter provides a powerful motive force, and Perdita's life in Bohemia associates her with flowers, fertility and harvest. When Leontes welcomes her and Florizel to Sicilia 'As is the spring to th'earth' (V.1.151), he is explicitly referring to the seasonal regeneration celebrated in the myth.

For Jacobean audiences, the play's mythological and Christian resonances would have worked side by side to create a profoundly spiritual impact without venturing into the dangerous waters of actual church doctrine.

Women in society

Despite the example of Queen Elizabeth I, Jacobean society remained firmly patriarchal and, in many respects, misogynistic. Women's choices

in time again — this time to 1940s America, its powerful political leaders presented as a cross between business tycoons and gangsters, and the square-dancing Bohemians redolent of the musical *Oklahoma!*

In David Farr's 2009 RSC production, the play's images of tales, texts and printing pervaded the design. The Sicilian court's towering bookcases were toppled by an earthquake at the climax of Act III to become the rugged Bohemian landscape. The bear was a huge puppet composed of torn pages, the satyr-dancers were costumed in shredded paper and Autolycus was festooned with ballad sheets. The director explained this as representing the collapse of civilised rationality, out of which grows a new generation. However, the *Sunday Telegraph* reviewer, Robert Gore-Langton, commented wryly, 'Oh, for a box of matches.'

That the play has survived such a diverse range of presentations is a testimony to Shakespeare's immense dramatic skill, frequently acknowledged by reviewers. In 2001, Nicholas de Jongh found that 'the superlative magic of the finale [worked] exhilarating wonders once again', while in 1999 Charles Spencer admitted: 'If I were forced to save only one Shakespeare play, I think my hand would hover over *Hamlet* and *King Lear* before finally opting for *The Winter's Tale*'.

Literary context

Sources of the play

The term 'sources' is perhaps a misleading one. It suggests that a writer creates a literary or dramatic work while surrounded by a variety of other texts, reshaping their plots, characters, ideas and language into something new and distinctive. Sometimes this is undoubtedly true, but sources often work in a less organised, more amorphous way, taking in memories and recollections, personal experience, contemporary cultural preoccupations and current events, in addition to the more specific influence of other plays, stories, poems and historical accounts.

In the narrow sense of the term, Shakespeare's principal source for *The Winter's Tale* is a prose romance by Robert Greene, probably first published in 1588, entitled *Pandosto: The Triumph of Time*. The subtitle suggests the author's moral or philosophical purpose, which is made more explicit further on in the title page: 'Although by the means of sinister fortune Truth may be concealed, yet by Time, in spite of fortune,

it is most manifestly revealed'. Later editions changed the title to *The History of Dorastus and Fawnia*, altering the focus from the jealous Pandosto (the equivalent of Leontes) to the young lovers, recreated by Shakespeare as Florizel and Perdita.

Why do scholars attach importance to an examination of Shakespeare's sources? This is a good question, since a text should surely stand by itself, able to be appreciated without reference to the influences that helped to shape it. Often, though, such a comparison can be revealing. Omissions, additions and changes of emphasis can help us to see something of Shakespeare's intentions and to appreciate the effects he created in fashioning a new work.

In *The Winter's Tale*, Shakespeare follows the essential storyline of *Pandosto* closely, and there are frequent echoes of Greene's language and phrasing. The overall effect of Shakespeare's play is quite different, however, as one would expect from a story that needs to be told in dramatic and theatrical terms through character and dialogue. Some of the key differences are outlined below.

- Shakespeare gives much greater emphasis and development to the two vitally contrasting emotional landscapes of his story: the jealousy of Leontes and the sheep-shearing celebrations, the latter developed from the merest hint in Greene. He also reverses the geographical settings, switching round Bohemia and Sicilia.

- Hermione's 'resurrection', the moving climax of Shakespeare's play, is his own invention. Her equivalent in *Pandosto*, Bellaria, genuinely dies after her trial; consequently, at the end of the story, after having been reunited with his daughter, there is no prospect of a new life for the repentant Pandosto, who commits suicide.

- Paulina, as stage-manager of Hermione's survival, therefore has no equivalent in Greene's story. She is one of the most memorable characters in the play and is entirely Shakespeare's.

- Other major characters added by Shakespeare are Antigonus and the Clown. Autolycus, whose amoral vitality is so crucial to the impact of the Bohemian scenes of the play, is also largely Shakespeare's invention. His roguery probably owes something to the rascals and vagabonds portrayed by Greene in his *Cony-Catching* pamphlets.

Shakespeare's resolution is only partly achieved by Time, and much more by the human qualities — love, loyalty and self-sacrifice — of characters such as Paulina, Camillo, Perdita and Florizel. Though Shakespeare adds a personification of Time as the chorus, he is an old-fashioned, partly comic, figure, reminding the audience of the old morality plays.

Task 11

Compare Robert Greene's *Pandosto* to *The Winter's Tale* (some editions of the play will include a copy of this source text). What do you feel are the most significant differences between the play and the prose romance in terms of form, structure and the treatment of central themes?

Critical context

Assessment Objective 3 requires you to demonstrate an understanding that the meaning of a text is not 'fixed', that at various places within a text different interpretations are possible. These different interpretations may be supported by reference to the ideas of named critics or particular critical perspectives, but may equally emerge from your own discussions with other students and your teacher. As indicated in the section on 'Working with AO3' (pp. 76–77 of this guide), what matters is that you have come to a personal interpretation of the play through an understanding of the different readings that are possible.

The section below outlines some significant ways in which *The Winter's Tale* has been interpreted since its earliest performance.

Interpretation in the past

The concept of Shakespeare's plays as objects of critical scrutiny did not really emerge until the eighteenth century. The gradually developing notion of Shakespeare's greatness led some critics to dismiss the plays they didn't like as either apprentice works, products of Shakespeare's dotage or the result of collaborations with inferior dramatists. In 1725, for example, Alexander Pope considered little of *The Winter's Tale* to be Shakespeare's.

With the Romantic period, in the early nineteenth century, came concepts of Shakespeare's genius, viewed as resembling some inexplicable natural force, plus a closer examination of his use of language. At various times since then, the focus of Shakespearean criticism has been on his stagecraft, his delineation of character and psychology, the mythic resonances of his plays and his use of imagery.

Criticism of *The Winter's Tale* has frequently seen it as part of the group of Shakespeare's final plays. Victorian critics often saw these works as exhibiting a serenity and tranquillity suggestive of a mellowing Shakespeare in semi-retirement. To some early twentieth-century critics, however, they demonstrated Shakespeare's boredom with drama and his interest only in fanciful poetry.

Neither of these views survives even a cursory study of the plays, and while the later assessment of them as experimental seems nearer to the truth, some critics have used this term as a sort of excuse for the plays perceived inadequacies.

*Pause for **Thought***

Consider the critic Lytton Strachey's view of the play, writing in 1922: 'It is difficult to resist the conclusion that [Shakespeare] was getting bored himself. Bored with people, bored with real life, bored with drama, bored, in fact, with everything except poetry and poetical dreams.'

Contemporary interpretation

Modern critical approaches can shed considerable light on the play.

Political criticism

Political criticism, which might include Marxist analysis and New Historicism, reminds us that literary texts are products of a particular set of socio-political circumstances from which they cannot be divorced, and that they are informed by a range of cultural preoccupations and anxieties that manifest themselves whether through the writer's concious intention or not. Politics plays more of a role in *The Winter's Tale* than is often recognised, for example in the portrait of two kings whose use and abuse of power forces them to confront issues of succession, responsible government and international alliances — issues that would be familiar to a Jacobean audience. The play, after all, was written at a time when the absolute power of the monarchy was being challenged by various groups within English society. It may be significant to note that it is the two kings who are presented at different times as offering the greatest threat to social and domestic harmony. Even the apparently apolitical figures of Autolycus and the Shepherd may represent familiar Jacobean social types: the first the potentially disruptive masterless man and sturdy beggar, and the second the economically savvy, rural entrepreneur, eager for social advancement.

Context

In contrast to these approaches, presentism is a more recent critical development that asserts that texts can only be read in the light of our own cultural circumstances, and we inevitably respond to them partly for the light they can shed on the world in which we live.

Madness and injustice in a king, as in Leontes' treatment of Hermione, were seen to threaten political stability. The trial scene from the Globe Theatre production, 1997.

TopFoto/UPP

Feminist criticism

Similarly, feminist criticism challenges assumptions about gender and exposes both the sexual stereotyping embodied in a text and the way in which such stereotypes might be subverted. Whether Shakespeare's plays exhibit feminist sympathies, or whether they merely accept and endorse the patriarchal status quo and misogyny of their time, is an issue that can only enhance a consideration of the roles of Hermione, Paulina and Perdita. It is certainly possible to argue that the three strongest characters in the play are all women. Their ability to confront and ultimately triumph over male weakness and hostility has been seen as demonstrating how the play challenges traditional gender stereotypes. An alternative feminist view is that the play upholds conventional male perspectives. Women are effectively sacrificed to resurrect male dominance. The final scene of the play, through this reading, presents Hermione as reduced to a re-animated statue, largely restricted in speech. Even Paulina has to be safely absorbed back into society through the male-dominated institution of marriage.

> It is certainly possible to argue that the three strongest characters in the play are all women

Performance criticism

This approach looks at how the form of dramatic texts is determined by their basis in theatrical practice, examining them against what is known of the original stage conditions for which they were produced and the way they have been represented subsequently in theatres and performance media (see 'Modern interpretations' under 'Cultural context', pp. 68–9 of this guide). It focuses on Shakespeare's stagecraft and the crucial elements of drama, such as words, movement, sound and costume. This approach questions the notion of a definitive text and undermines the concept of authorship, as theatre is essentially collaborative and ephemeral.

Psychoanalytic criticism

This type of criticism examines the significance of the subconscious as a means of exploring the representation of character. Much psychoanalytical criticism is based on the theories of Sigmund Freud, and explores the effect of dreams, fantasies, unconscious desires and aspects of sexuality. Freudian readings of the play have focused on the nature and origins of Leontes' jealousy, at times suggesting that the boyhood friendship of Leontes and Polixenes generated an intensity of feeling that was later threatened by Leontes' marriage to Hermione. Other areas of *The Winter's Tale* that lend themselves to psychoanalytic readings include father-son relationships, dreams and nightmares, and the overtly sexual nature of much of the imagery of the play.

Working with the text

The first and most important thing to remember is that the text itself will lie at the heart of your study, whether you are studying the play for coursework or for examination. Therefore, although you may need to become familiar with such elements of the course as the format and style of examination questions and the four Assessment Objectives, nothing will be as significant as your own close knowledge of the text.

The second important thing to remember is the importance of relevance. Whether the question you are required to answer is on an examination paper or a coursework task, you will be given little credit for including material that is of limited relevance to the question.

Finally, expect to have to approach the text in different ways, depending on the form of your examination response. Traditional coursework and controlled conditions assessment, open and closed book examinations, conventional literary analysis and re-creative or transformational writing, studied or unseen texts all require distinctively different approaches which you will have to prepare for carefully with your teacher.

Meeting the Assessment Objectives

The four key English literature Assessment Objectives (AOs) describe the different skills you need to show in order to get a good grade. Regardless of what texts or what examination specification you are following, the AOs lie at the heart of your study of English literature at AS and A2; they let you know exactly what the examiners are looking for and provide a helpful framework for your literary studies.

The Assessment Objectives require you to:
- articulate creative, informed and relevant responses to literary texts, using appropriate terminology and concepts, and coherent, accurate written expression (AO1)

- demonstrate detailed critical understanding in analysing the ways in which structure, form and language shape meanings in literary texts (AO2)

- explore connections and comparisons between different literary texts, informed by interpretations of other readers (AO3)

- demonstrate understanding of the significance and influence of the contexts in which literary texts are written and understood (AO4)

Try to bear in mind that the AOs are there to support rather than restrict you; don't look at them as encouraging a tick-box approach or a mechanistic, reductive way into the study of literature. Examination questions are written with the AOs in mind, so if you answer them clearly and carefully you should automatically hit the right targets. If you are devising your own questions for coursework, seek the help of your teacher to ensure that your essay title is carefully worded to liberate the required AOs so that you can do your best.

Although the Assessment Objectives are common to all the exam boards, each specification varies enormously in the way they meet the requirements. The boards' websites provide useful information, including sections for students, past papers, sample papers and mark schemes.

AQA: **www.aqa.org.uk**

Edexcel: **www.edexcel.com**

OCR: **www.ocr.org.uk**

WJEC: **www.wjec.co.uk**

Working with AO1

AO1 focuses upon literary and critical insight, organisation of material and clarity of written communication. Examiners are looking for accurate spelling and grammar, and clarity of thought and expression, so say what you want to say, and say it as clearly as you can. Aim for cohesion; your ideas should be presented coherently with an overall sense of a developing argument. Try to use 'appropriate terminology' but don't hide behind fancy critical terms or complicated language you don't fully understand; 'feature-spotting' and merely listing literary terms is a classic banana skin all examiners are familiar with. Choose your references carefully; copying out great gobbets of a text learned by heart underlines your inability to select the choicest short quotation with which to clinch your argument. The hallmarks of a well-written essay — whether for coursework or in an exam — include a clear and coherent

introduction that orientates the reader, a systematic and logical argument, aptly chosen and neatly embedded quotations and a conclusion which consolidates your case.

Working with AO2

In studying any text you should think about its overall form (novel, sonnet, tragedy, farce etc.), structure (how it is organised, how its constituent parts connect with each other) and language. In studying *The Winter's Tale* it might be just as useful to begin with the larger elements of form and structure before considering language. If 'form is meaning', what are the implications of categorising *The Winter's Tale* as a tragicomedy or a romance? The play is structured in a very distinctive way, as further explored in 'Structure' in the *Form, structure and language* section (pp. 55–57 of this guide). There has been much debate about the dramatic effectiveness of some aspects of this structure. In terms of language features, what is most striking about the diction of the play —dialogue, soliloquy, imagery or symbolism?

In order to discuss language in detail you will need to quote from the text — but the mere act of quoting is not enough to meet AO2. What is important is what you do with the quotation — how you analyse it and use it to illuminate your argument. Moreover, since you will at times need to make points about larger generic and organisational features of the play, such as the relationship between acts or scenes which are much too long to quote, being able to reference effectively is just as important as mastering the art of the embedded quotation.

Working with AO3

AO3 is a double Assessment Objective which asks you to 'explore connections and comparisons' between texts as well as to show your understanding of the views and interpretations of others.

Connections and comparisons

You will find it easier to make comparisons and connections between texts (of any kind) if you try to balance them as you write; remember also that connections and comparisons are not only about finding similarities — differences are just as interesting. Above all, consider how the comparison illuminates each text. It is not just a matter of finding the relationships and connections but of analysing what they show.

Some connections will be thematic, others generic or stylistic. There are many ways in which *The Winter's Tale* can be compared to the other Shakespearean 'last plays', such as *Pericles* or *The Tempest*, in terms of form, structure, language and theme. *Othello* provides a contrasting dramatic study of jealousy. If you wish to explore thematic contrasts across different literary genres, in Mark Twain's *Huckleberry Finn* young people also escape from a corrupted adult society into a pastoral world. Evelyn Waugh's *A Handful of Dust*, in contrast, presents an urban, sophisticated world of very real infidelity, but the contrasting pastoral culture proves to offer an even more macabre form of imprisonment.

Showing understanding of the views and interpretations of others

To access the second half of AO3 effectively, you need to measure your own interpretation of a text against those of your teacher and other students. By all means refer to named critics and quote from them if it seems appropriate, but the examiners are most interested in your personal and creative response. If your teacher takes a particular critical line, be prepared to challenge and question it; there is nothing more dispiriting for an examiner than to read a set of scripts from one centre which all say exactly the same thing. Top candidates produce fresh personal responses rather than merely regurgitating the ideas of others, however famous or insightful their interpretations may be. *The Winter's Tale* has generated widely differing responses ever since it was first staged. It thus lends itself readily to a range of interpretations, some of which are indicated in the section on 'Critical context' (pp. 71–73 of this guide). Critical debate, for instance, has often focused on the supposed awkwardness of the play's structure, or the degree to which the onset of Leontes' jealousy and Hermione's resurrection are dramatically convincing.

Try to show an awareness of multiple readings with regard to the play and an understanding that its meaning is dependent as much upon what the audience brings to it as what Shakespeare left there. Using modal verb phrases such as 'may be seen as', 'might be interpreted as' or 'could be represented as' implies that you are aware that different readers interpret texts in different ways at different times. The key word here is plurality; there is no single meaning, no right answer, and you need to evaluate a range of other ways of making textual meanings as you work towards your own.

> Top candidates produce fresh personal responses rather than merely regurgitating the ideas of others

Working with AO4

AO4, with its emphasis on the 'significance and influence' of the 'contexts in which literary texts are written and received', might at first seem less deeply rooted in the text itself but in fact you are considering and evaluating here the relationship between the text and its contexts. Note the word 'received': this refers to the way interpretation can be influenced by the specific contexts within which the reader is operating; when you are studying a text written many years ago, there is often an immense gulf between the original contemporary context and the twenty-first century context in which you receive it.

To access AO4 successfully, you need to think about how contexts of production, reception, literature, culture, biography, geography, society, history, genre and intertextuality can affect texts. Place the play at the heart of the web of contextual factors which you feel have had the most impact upon it; examiners want to see a sense of contextual alertness woven seamlessly into the fabric of your essay rather than a clumsy 'bolted-on' rehash of a website or your old history notes. Try to convey your awareness of the fact that literary works contain embedded and encoded representations of the cultural, moral, religious, racial and political values of the society from which they emerged, and that over time attitudes and ideas change until the views they reflect are no longer widely shared. You would be right to think that there must be an overlap between a focus on interpretations (AO3) and a focus on contexts, so don't worry about pigeonholing the AOs here.

Further discussion of some contexts relevant to *The Winter's Tale* can be found in the *Contexts* section (pp. 61–73 of this guide).

Approaching different types of written response

Extended commentaries

In order to respond effectively to AO2, whether in examination essay or coursework, you need to show that you can analyse form, structure and language in detail. Select some key passages from the play and practise analysing them, as well as setting them in the wider context of the whole play. Below is an example of the sort of analysis you might carry out.

Sample commentary

This is an extended commentary on Act I scene 2, lines 284–318 ('Is whispering nothing'...'draught to me were cordial').

By this stage of the play, Leontes has convinced himself that his wife has been unfaithful to him with Polixenes. He has also attempted to convince Camillo of the truth of his suspicions.

Leontes' jealousy, which dominates this scene, is revealed as obsessive and wholly self-inflicted. This provides a telling contrast with Shakespeare's tragedy *Othello,* where the central protagonist has his mind poisoned against his wife by his villainous subordinate Iago. Here, Leontes' attendant lord, Camillo, attempts to dissuade the king from his rash course of action. Other voices in the play later prove equally helpless in the face of the king's folly. Leontes is to bring his fall on himself.

This idea of a fall allows us to see the form of the play as, in part at least, a tragedy. The genre of the whole play is often thought of as a tragicomedy, in that the full potential impact of tragedy is averted and the forces of life and reconciliation reclaim the characters from the threat of death. In this section of the play, however, Shakespeare is exploring aspects of the tragic experience.

In the sense that there are two characters on stage who are talking to each other, this section of the scene is clearly structured around dialogue, but a dialogue which is strikingly unbalanced. Leontes dominates the scene. Before this extract Camillo has indignantly defended the queen. Now he is reduced first to helpless denials 'No, no, my lord' and then to bewildered questions 'Who does infect her?' Meanwhile Leontes rants on. It is almost as if he is hardly conscious of a listener. In some ways, his speeches here almost act as soliloquies, as they have in his earlier conversation with Mamillius.

The repeated and insistent questions which open this extract (284–92) follow each other so quickly that they allow no time for a response. In fact, Leontes requires no response. He answers his questions himself, thus implying that the answer is too obvious to require a reply 'Is this nothing?/Why then the world and all that's in't, is nothng.'

Leontes' twisted state of mind is revealed through other aspects of his language. The broken verse rhythms of lines 308–316 almost make Leontes' thoughts unintelligible. The whole of this speech (307–18) is one long sentence in which clause becomes embedded in clause and phrase overlaps phrase so that the listener becomes bewildered in attempting to follow the jagged course of the king's argument. The lines more or less keep to the iambic metre, but the grammatical structures break across these verse patterns. Meaning concludes in the middle of a line (308) and enjambement constantly pulls meaning across from one line to another 'they would do that/ Which should undo more doing': Leontes' language, like his mind, is in conflict with itself.

A clear pattern to Leontes' speech is provided, however, by his obsessive repetitions. The opening words 'Is whispering nothing?' build to a crazed climax where his speech is reduced to a series of 'nothings'. Eight times the word is used as the king's hysterical repetition creates both dramatic intensity and a sense that his world now has lost meaning.

This sense of the growing meaningless of Leontes' existence reflects his tragic status and the precipitate nature of his fall. Shakespeare's tragic protagonist Macbeth, conscious of his approaching destruction, comes to a similarly nihilistic view: 'Life's but a walking shadow…a tale/Told by an idiot, full of sound and fury,/Signifying nothing.'

The imagery of Leontes' speech is equally revealing. A dominant cluster of images within the play involves ideas of disease, sickness and cure. Leontes, obsessed with the thought of his wife's infidelity, sees her whole life as 'infected'. 'Who does infect her?' asks the bewildered Camillo. Leontes then proceeds to identify Polixenes as the source of her infection: 'he that wears her like her medal'. The simile at the heart of this accusation has the additional impact of reducing Hermione to the status of a trophy.

Camillo, however, sees Leontes as the one who is truly sick: 'Good my lord, be cured/Of this diseased opinion.' It is the king who is diseased and in need of cure; Leontes is represented as a source of infection within a healthy court. His sickness is further demonstrated by the reversal of values revealed in his claim that a poisoned cup presented to Polixenes would act (to Leontes) as a 'cordial'.

In a play where death and destruction follow from the king's inability to see clearly, images of 'eyes' and 'seeing' are understandably persistent. Leontes deludes himself that all eyes but his are 'blind with pin and web' (which also, in its reference to cataracts, presents another image of sickness). He accuses Camillo of failing to make clear judgements: 'with thine eyes at once see good and evil,/Inclining to them both'.

The same accusation is wildly levelled at all his other servants: they lack 'eyes/To see alike mine honour as their profits'. Only Leontes, it seems, sees 'Plainly as heaven sees earth and earth sees heaven'. The king's ludicrous over-estimation of his own perception carries with it some of the arrogance that is often characteristic of the Shakespearean tragic protagonist. Leontes speaks of killing Polixenes in terms of giving him 'a lasting wink', closing his eyes for ever, but it is Leontes who is blind, and his later regaining of his sight will only come at a terrible cost.

Coursework essays

Whatever coursework task you choose, ensure that it clearly addresses the relevant Assessment Objectives and allows for adequate, focused treatment within the given word limits. There are a number of key stages in the coursework writing process:

- Choose your title and discuss it with your teacher as soon as possible.
- Set aside an hour to jot down ideas for the essay and convert them into an essay plan. Share this plan with your teacher and make use of any feedback offered.
- Identify any background reading, such as textual criticism, that may be useful to you, gather the books you need, read them and make notes.
- Give yourself a reasonable period to draft the essay, working with your text, your notes and other useful materials around you.
- Keep referring back to the title or question, and make sure that you remain focused on it.
- Allow time for your teacher to read and comment on at least part of your draft.
- Redraft your essay until you are satisfied with it. Keep checking that you have focused on the relevant Assessment Objectives.
- A bibliography will add to the professionalism of your essay. This should list all the texts you have quoted from and consulted. Check with your teacher whether you are required to use any particular format for a bibliography, and do not deviate from it.
- Proof-read your essay carefully before handing it in.

Suggested titles

1 **How does Shakespeare portray the women in the play? Examine the characterisation and role of the female characters.**

2 **Does Shakespeare succeed in individualising the minor characters so as to make them interesting parts to act as well**

as contributing to the dramatic effects of the play? Consider four or five examples to support your answer. (Suggestions: Archidamus; Cleomenes and Dion; Emilia; Mamillius; Mopsa and Dorcas; the Shepherd's servant; the three Gentlemen.)

3 How has your understanding of the play been enhanced by your reading of a variety of literary criticism? What critical views have you encountered that you consider particularly interesting, revealing or controversial?

4 How successfully do you think *The Winter's Tale* works as a text for the theatre?

Some ideas for tackling essay 4

- exploitation of indoor facilities of Blackfriars Theatre, while remaining appropriate for outdoor performance at the Globe

- analysis of overall structure of the play: tragedy, comedy, resolution; the two worlds of Sicilia and Bohemia

- some comment on principal themes of the play and the imagery that supports them, relating this to both structure and genre

- relevance of the play's portrayal of monarchy and rural life to contemporary and twenty-first century social and political ideas, e.g. the issue of succession; women's place in society; art and nature; social divisions; attitudes to rogues and vagabonds

- the kind of characters in the play, the dramatic effectiveness of the characterisation and the possibilities for actors to realise the characters in performance

- dramatic qualities of the play, especially the use of contrast between high drama, low comedy, idealised romance, spectacular moments, music and song, masque-like elements, verse and prose etc.

- effect on the audience, e.g. how dramatic, funny, moving the play is; which parts work best, which are less successful: consider how you think the members of the audience should feel as they leave a good production of the play

Exam essays

As always with examination questions, ensure that you select your question carefully from the available options and identify all of the key words in the question. Check carefully to see if you are required to argue a case around a particular interpretation of the play. Ensure that you know exactly what sections of the text and contextual materials are likely to be relevant to the chosen question.

Whole-text questions

You can use the questions below for examination practice. You can also use them to provide ideas for class debate, individual research, or group presentations. (This also, of course, applies to other questions provided in this guide.)

1 **What elements of social and political awareness have you found in *The Winter's Tale*?**

2 **Are Florizel and Perdita any more than idealised romantic lovers?**

3 **Examine two or three of the prose sections in the play. Consider aspects of Shakespeare's prose style, suggest why these sections are in prose and not verse, and assess their impact in the dramatic context.**

4 **Do you think *The Winter's Tale* offers a stereotypical view of women, or does it challenge women's traditional role in society?**

Possible ideas to include in a plan for essay 4
Introduction:

● views of Shakespeare's female characters have changed from century to century as women's social status has changed

● Victorian critics, for example, tended to idealise Hermione, Paulina and Perdita as emblems of noble and selfless womanhood: courageous, dignified, patient, loyal and forgiving

● in our century we can be aware of elements of female stereotypes in the characters, but also see them as a critique of such stereotyping

Stereotypes:

● the three central women fall into particular stereotypes: the nagging scold, the victimised wife, the beautiful princess

● Mopsa and Dorcas are also stereotyped as jealous rivals

● Paulina especially is defined by Leontes as shrewish wife and even witch (see Act II scene 3)

● Shakespeare allows the women themselves to refer to anti-feminist stereotypes — see II.1.108–09, III.2.217–18 and V.3.89–91

● Perdita's association with flowers seems to make her an emblem of fragile beauty

● other women are either impotent victims of patriarchal power (Hermione's ladies, Antigonus's daughters) or models of domesticity (Shepherd's wife)

- all the play's major actions are initiated by men; the women merely respond

Stereotypes challenged:

- despite the above, it is the women of the play who are the characters we admire — in varying degrees they stand up against male tyranny
- they are not idealised, however, but given human weaknesses and errors of judgement: Hermione fails to read Leontes' state of mind, Paulina leaves the baby unprotected
- Perdita's flower speeches could be interpreted as suggestive of strength, e.g. the power and vigour of the daffodils
- the play's regenerative outcome is entirely due to female power and management of events

Possible conclusion:

Shakespeare's intentions are unknown to us. We have to make our own interpretations of the text we are given. What we can say is that the text offers opportunities to see its women as subversive of patriarchal stereotypes.

Extract-based essay questions

When tackling passage-based analysis, depending on the precise nature of the question, you might consider the points outlined below:

- Is the section in prose, verse or a mixture of the two? What is notable about the way these language modes are used?
- What is its place in the development of the plot?
- What is going on between the characters present, and what is the impact of any entrances and exits?
- What is the impact of characters who say little in the section?
- How does the language of the scene reveal character?
- What is the balance between dialogue and soliloquy, longer and shorter speeches?
- How does the section support the wider imagery and themes of the play?
- What is the function of the given section in the dramatic structure of the play? Are there any parallels or contrasts with other episodes? What would the play lose without this section?

Sample questions could include the following:

1 Write an analysis of Act I scene 1. How effectively does it begin the play?

2 **How does Shakespeare change the mood and tone of the play in the second half of Act III scene 3, lines 58–119?**

3 **Reread Act IV scene 4, lines 70–135. What impression of Perdita is created in her flower speeches?**

Approaching a comparative essay

AO3 requires you to explore connections and comparisons between different literary texts. The extract below from a student's essay, involving a comparison between *The Winter's Tale* and a text from a different literary genre, demonstrates some ways in which this AO may be effectively delivered.

Sample A-grade essay

Compare and contrast the ways in which Shakespeare and Shelley present parent–child relationships in *The Winter's Tale* (c. 1611) and *Frankenstein* (1818).

The relationships between Leontes and Perdita, and Victor Frankenstein and the monster he creates are fundamental to *The Winter's Tale* and *Frankenstein*. Both texts deal with abandoned children offspring who are set apart by the mysterious circumstances surrounding their births, but while the abandoned Perdita is raised by a kind foster-father who welcomes her into a new family, the creature is marginalised and rejected by society.**1**

Generically, while *Frankenstein* is not only a novel of Gothic horror but also a psychological journey and mythic fable, *The Winter's Tale* is a dramatic tragicomedy or romance, often categorised with other late Shakespearean plays such as *The Tempest* and *Pericles*. A significant feature of such tragicomedies is that the central characters do not suffer death.**2**

In Robert Greene's *Pandosto*, the source Shakespeare used for *The Winter's Tale*, both main characters, the king and queen, die.**3** However, in Shakespeare's text both Leontes and Hermione survive and get a second chance at happiness. In *The Winter's Tale* the tragedy has a clear cut-off point, in Act III scene 3, in the centre of the play. Here the evil that befalls the innocent in Sicilia ends and others begin to undo the damage caused by Leontes' jealousy. Significantly this dramatic shift**4** is marked by the Shepherd's discovery of Perdita, whose name means 'the lost one', the daughter Leontes wanted to have killed. After Antigonus's macabre death is described by the Clown, the Shepherd changes the tone of the play completely, telling his son, 'Thou met'st with things dying, I with things new born' (III.3.100–01).

1 A tight, convincing link is established between the two texts (AO3).

2 Moves from a general identification of genre features to a close application to the first text (AO4).

3 A lucid, cohesive argument is being developed (AO1).

4 Clear sense of dramatic structure here (AO2).

This structural turning point allows the audience to compare a series of binary opposites**5** such as death and birth, disease and recovery, and winter and spring. After the jealous madness of Perdita's real father and the tragic death of her brother Mamillius, Shakespeare introduces a substitute father and brother for her, the Shepherd and the Clown. 'I'll take it up for pity,' says the Shepherd when he finds her, and even 16 years later**6** his care for and pride in her are evident. When her dancing is praised he answers: 'So she does any thing, though I report it that should be silent.' Dramatically the Shepherd's discovery of the child creates the impression that the worst is over**7**, and the subsequent onstage action follows a pathway of redemption, recovery and resolution. Significantly Perdita, who represents Leontes' only chance to redeem himself, is 'a goodly babe/Lusty and like to live'. (II.2.26–27)

In *The Winter's Tale* Perdita is marginalised because of her real or supposed illegitimacy, yet she remains a force for good. Conversely in *Frankenstein* the creature, rejected by society because of his appearance, turns to evil. Shelley uses the creature to dramatise her argument that when people are treated brutally, they become brutal themselves. This builds on the French philosopher Jean-Jacques Rousseau's idea of the 'noble savage' who is born innocent and corrupted by society.**8** As she was married to an atheist and was the daughter of a radical philosopher and arch-feminist, Shelley may well have doubted the existence of God. Her use of the epigraph**9** from Milton's *Paradise Lost*, 'Did I request thee, Maker, from my clay/To mould Me man? Did I solicit thee/from darkness to promote Me?' suggests that the creature has lost his faith and wishes he had never been born. I agree with Sandra Gilbert's analysis of the creature's embedded narrative as an expression of 'existentialist agony' buried at the heart of the text like the cry of a lost and frightened child.**10**

Whereas Perdita, although initially an abandoned outcast, grows up loved, secure and happy, the creature is cruelly abused and mistreated.**11** In the Open University programme *Building the Perfect Beast*, the feminist critic Sandra Gilbert describes the creature's embedded tale as 'Eve's narrative' — the story of one cast out of paradise by a controlling male force and doomed to suffer for ever, unable to return to a state of innocence. The creature's narrative, furthermore, is also interlinked with another narrator's, as he shares the telling of the story with two other narrators. In this, as in other ways, the creature is not allowed full control of his own history.**12**

Structurally both texts are extremely interesting in other ways. The famous frame narrative and Russian doll layering of *Frankenstein* (in which Walton's letters to his sister enclose Victor's story, with the creature's narrative at the heart of the text) mirror the patchwork creation of the creature itself. *The Winter's Tale* has been seen as a 'broken-backed' play artificially split in two by the appearance of Time to represent the passage of 16 years, but these years are the period during which Perdita grows from infancy to womanhood. In both texts, therefore, the narrative structure is significantly tied to the development of the complex relationship between parent and child.

In terms of setting, *Frankenstein* is set against an icy and isolated landscape, which may represent parts of the human mind over which we have little control. The meeting of Victor and the creature on the lonely *Mer de Glace* and their final fates in the frozen Arctic are psychologically very convincing — it seems right that father and son face each other at the extreme edge of the earth. Shakespeare's 'mistake' in giving landlocked Bohemia a sea-coast has been pointed out for centuries, but it can be seen as adding another layer of unreality and fantasy to the other fantastic, supernatural and non-naturalistic elements of *The Winter's Tale* such as the figure of Time, the intervention of the Delphic oracle and the final 'moving statue' scene. There is, however, enough in Bohemia that is firmly anchored in a realistic rural world to allow Perdita to appear as not only a semi-mythical representation of fertility, but also a woman whose unsophisticated virtues have much to teach the twisted, inward-looking world of her father.

This is only the first half of the original essay, but there should be enough here to show you how the essay satisfies all the criteria for a top-band mark.

Examiner's comments

AO1: A fluent, articulate and well-structured argument. Critical vocabulary is appropriately used.

AO2: There is a detailed exploration and analysis of form, structure and language, with confident evaluation of how they shape meanings.

AO3: Convincing connections and comparisons between texts lie firmly at the heart of the argument. A sensitive understanding of different possible readings of the texts is clearly demonstrated.

AO4: The relationship between the texts, the task and the contexts, cultural, historical and other, is explored and evaluated.

More sample essays are included on the free website at **www.philipallan.co.uk/literatureguidesonline**

Transformational tasks

Transformative writing (sometimes called re-creative writing) requires you to demonstrate understanding of the text from a different perspective from that offered by a conventional academic essay. You might explore a reading of the text through using the voice of a relatively minor character, provide a different interpretation of events from that delivered in the original text, or look at a 'gap' in the original story and fill that gap through an additional piece of narrative. You may be required, in addition, to write a commentary in which you explain some of the significant decisions you made in creating the new text. Below are some possible ways in which a transformative writing approach might be applied to *The Winter's Tale*.

1 **There are many occasions in the play where we are not given Paulina's response to events or allowed to hear important conversations. Either (a) write a monologue, delivered by Paulina, when she hears that her husband has been ordered by Leontes to take Hermione's daughter away and expose the child to probable death. Or (b) write one or more extracts from conversations between Paulina and Hermione during the time when the queen is in hiding. Ensure that you create a voice or voices appropriate to the original characters.**

2 **Write two obituaries or eulogies to Hermione from two different points of view, delivered soon after her supposed death. Consider carefully the difference in the viewpoints provided and use an appropriate register in your writing.**

3 **Write two extracts from Camillo's diary, written during his voyages from and to Sicilia. Make the language as well as the content of the diary entries reflect your reading of Camillo's character and role.**

Top ten quotations

Look carefully at the following quotations and consider the different ways in which they are significant within the play. How might they be used in an essay to help an exploration of different elements or readings of *The Winter's Tale*? Consider questions of language and structure, aspects of dramatic presentation, revelation of character, important themes and different critical interpretations of the play.

Ten 'top' quotations have been identified here, but you may find others that are of similarly wide significance. Whichever you use, ensure that they are carefully integrated into your argument and not merely left hanging as little more than decoration.

> **He makes a July's day short as December,**
> **And with his varying childness cures in me**
> **Thoughts that would thick my blood.**   **(I.2.169–71)**

1

Polixenes is talking about his son, and links him to the contrasting seasons, an idea to become more important later. The idea of the rejuvenating, curative power of youth is also suggested. Ironically, Mamillius cannot perform the same function for Leontes.

> **Inch-thick, knee-deep; o'er head and ears a forked one.**
> **Go, play, boy, play: thy mother plays, and I**
> **Play too — but so disgraced a part whose issue**
> **Will hiss me to my grave..**   **(I.2.186–89)**

2

Leontes here shows his growing sexual obsession: 'forked one' indicates his fear that he has become a cuckold, but it could also suggest demonic behaviour. The central idea of 'playing' is indicated. Hermione is seen as flirtatiously 'playing'; however, the playing of Mamillius is innocent. Leontes' 'play' is an illusion; he has created for himself a fictitious role, another example of the dominant idea within *The Winter's Tale* of role-play, acting a part. Leontes feels he has been disgraced, but ironically his real disgrace is to follow.

> **...This action I now go on**
> **Is for my better grace. Adieu, my lord.**
> **I never wished to see you sorry; now**
> **I trust I shall.**   **(II.1.121–24)**

3

Hermione's language, measured, calm and balanced, provides a striking contrast with Leontes' tortured syntax. She is associated with the central idea of grace (see I.1.105 and compare Leontes' disgrace). Some readers may find her submissive passivity unattractive; others may see it as raising her above the petty world of Leontes' suspicions.

> **I am a feather for each wind that blows.**
> **Shall I live on to see this bastard kneel**
> **And call me father?**   **(II.3.153–55)**

4

Leontes here seems tyrannical, but at the same time strangely weak, as insubstantial as a 'feather'. Both externally and internally he is constantly wavering and insecure. The spitting out of the word 'bastard' damns him as a cruel and inadequate father, but ironically his words also anticipate what will happen. He will 'live on' until Perdita returns.

5

> **A thousand knees,**
> **Ten thousand years together, naked, fasting,**
> **Upon a barren mountain, and still winter**
> **In storm perpetual, could not move the gods**
> **To look that way thou wert.** (III.2.207–11)

Here we see something of Paulina's dramatic function. She acts as Leontes' conscience, but also as his accuser, exacting punishment. Note the stress on time, here signifying eternal pain, and winter. The gods have absented themselves from Leontes' world. The language, characteristic of the first half of the play, is full of exaggeration and excess.

6

> **Thou met'st with things dying, I with things new born.**
> (III.3.100–02)

This is commonly recognised as a pivotal line in the overall structure of the play. The world of tragedy is about to slip into comedy. The death of Antigonus precedes the saving of Perdita's life; age meets youth; winter will turn to spring.

7

> **...Impute it not a crime**
> **To me or my swift passage that I slide**
> **O'er sixteen years...** (IV.1.4–6)

This is an indication of the complex dramatic function of Time, a symbolic figure variously represented on stage in different dramatic productions. He acts as a device to speed up the action, enable growth and provide the possibility of renewal. The audience is directly addressed in formal, rhetorical language. We have a more than human force at work here.

8

> **Come, take your flowers.**
> **Methinks I play as I have seen them do**
> **In Whitsun pastorals; sure this robe of mine**
> **Does change my disposition.** (IV.4.132–35)

The key word 'play' occurs here again, but in a very different context. Perdita is associated with the spring festival of Whitsun and with the flowers that she distributes. She is both transformed by her role and the agent of others' transformation.

9

> **Such a deal of wonder is broken out within this hour that**
> **ballad-makers cannot be able to express it....This news,**

> which is called true, is so like an old tale that the verity of
> it is in strong suspicion. (V.2.19–24)

This is an interesting example of Shakespeare's use of prose dialogue within the play. Here the Gentlemen are used to delay and anticipate the final reconciliation scene by reporting offstage action. The rather artificial nature of the choric device is cheerfully acknowledged 'like an old tale', an idea which has run through the play. Words like 'wonder' encourage and shape audience reaction. Soon we will be invited to suspend our disbelief further.

10

> Music; awake her; strike.
> 'Tis time; descend; be stone no more; approach;
> Strike all that look upon with marvel. Come;
> I'll fill your grave up. (V.3.98–101)

The dramatic use of music here accompanies significant action. Paulina uses short, insistent, imperative phrases to direct the scene. 'Marvel' continues the sense of wonder. Hermione and those who watch emerge from a dream. Death is defeated through an act of 'natural' magic. The power of art to transform nature is celebrated and tragedy turns to harmony and rebirth.

Taking it further

Editions of the play

All good editions of *The Winter's Tale* contain useful notes and stimulating introductions. Some of the best are listed below.

- Innes, S. and Huddlestone, E. (eds) (1998) *Cambridge School Shakespeare, The Winter's Tale*, Cambridge University Press
  - This is the edition that has been used for the textual references in this guide
- O'Connor, J. (ed.) (2003) *New Longman Shakespeare*, Longman
- Orgel, S. (ed.) (1996) *The Oxford Shakespeare*, Clarendon Press
- Pafford, J. H. P. (ed.) (1963) *The Arden Shakespeare*, 2nd series, Methuen
- Schanzer, E. (ed.) (1969) *The New Penguin Shakespeare*, Penguin

Criticism of the play

- Batholomeusz, D. (1982) *The Winter's Tale in Performance in England and America, 1611–1976*, Cambridge University Press
  - An overview of the performance history of the play that provides some insight into different interpretations
- Hussey, S. (1992) *The Literary Language of Shakespeare*, Longman
  - An interesting exploration of some of the features of language used in Shakespeare's plays, with an interesting chapter on *The Winter's Tale*
- Kermode, F. (2000) *Shakespeare's Language*, Allen Lane, Penguin
  - A study of the development of Shakespeare's dramatic language, with a chapter on the linguistic range of *The Winter's Tale*
- Muir, K. (ed.) (1969) *Shakespeare: The Winter's Tale*, Casebook Series, Macmillan
  - A wide selection of different critical responses to the play, from the seventeenth to the twentieth century
- Overton, B. (1989) *The Winter's Tale, The Critics Debate*, Macmillan
  - An overview of recent critical approaches to the play and some discussion of significant dramatic issues

Criticism of Shakespeare's last plays

All three of the books below, though dating from the middle of the twentieth century, are still well worth a look.

- Tillyard, E. M. W. (1938) *Shakespeare's Last Plays*, Chatto and Windus
  - A good example of a traditional critical approach that sees the plays as considerable dramatic achievements
- Traversi, D. (1954) *Shakespeare: The Last Phase*, Hollis and Carter
  - Argues that *The Winter's Tale* represents a considerable advance on the earlier 'late plays', and explores the symphonic nature of the play's structure
- Wilson Knight, G. (1947) *The Crown of Life*, Oxford University Press (repr. Methuen, 1965)
  - Another positive critical view of the play, with an emphasis on the quality of the play's language

Context

- Bate, J. (2008) *The Genius of Shakespeare*, Picador

- A very useful text for contextualising Shakespeare's life and work. A wide-ranging and lively book
- Dusinberre, J. (1996) *Shakespeare and the Nature of Women*, Macmillan
  - One of the first and still most-read feminist readings of the plays. Considers, among other perspectives, how the play satirises women
- Gurr, A. (1992) *The Shakespearean Stage 1574–1642*, 3rd edn, Cambridge University Press
  - A standard and comprehensive guide to theatre history
- McEvoy, S. (2000) *Shakespeare: The Basics*, Routledge
  - A good example of how an exploration of social and cultural contexts can inform a reading of the play

Films

The Winter's Tale has not proved popular with film-makers. The following, however, are available on DVD:

1981: BBC production directed by Jane Howell with Anna Calder-Marshall as Hermione and Jeremy Kemp as Leontes; available as a BBC DVD.

2000: RSC production directed by Gregory Doran recorded at the Barbican Theatre with Antony Sher as Leontes and Alexandra Gilbreath as Hermione; available as a Heritage Theatre DVD. There is also a separate production casebook, also on Heritage Theatre DVD, with extracts from the production interspersed with a variety of interviews with the cast and production team.

Other films include:

1962: BBC production directed by Don Taylor with Robert Shaw as Leontes.

1968: directed by Frank Dunlop, featuring Laurence Harvey, Jane Asher and Jim Dale.

Audio

Various audio versions of the play are available, including:

- Arkangel, featuring Sinead Cusack and Ciaran Hinds (CD and cassette)
- HarperCollins, featuring Peggy Ashcroft and John Gielgud (cassette)
- Caedmon Shakespeare, narrated by John Gielgud (CD)

Internet

There is so much Shakespeare material available on the internet that it is difficult to know what is likely to be useful and reliable. The following are worth investigating:

- **http://shakespeare.palomar.edu** is entitled *Mr William Shakespeare and the Internet* and aims to be a complete, annotated scholarly guide to all the Shakespeare resources available online.
- **http://www.rsc.org.uk** is the Royal Shakespeare Company's website.
- **http://www.shakespearesglobe.org** is the official website of the reconstructed Globe Theatre.
- **http://www.shakespeare.org.uk** The Shakespeare Centre Library in Stratford-upon-Avon houses the archive of the Royal Shakespeare Company, where you can look up the records of all Stratford productions of *The Winter's Tale*, including prompt-books, photographs and press cuttings. Small groups or individual students can also arrange to watch videos of productions since the early 1980s. Recorded in performance with a fixed camera, the visual quality of these is sometimes poor, but they are useful records of how the play was staged and acted. Find out more via the website.